Now, I See

Madelyn March

CreateSpace
Pinckney, Michigan

Publisher's Note: This is a work of fiction. Names, characters, places, and incidents are a product of the author's imagination. Locales and public names are sometimes used for atmospheric purposes. Any resemblance to actual people, living or dead, or to businesses, companies, events, institutions, or locales is completely coincidental.

Now, I See/ Madelyn March -- 1st ed.
ISBN 978-1547295944

Cover Design by Ana Grigoria at Books-design.com

To The Muse Crew

The Change

I remember some things. I remember walking down Maple Street in Chicago, the sloshing sound of late-winter slush under my boots and the cold phone against my ear. I remember the words my father uttered that changed me. What I don't remember is how I got from that cold moment to sitting in my father's overheated living room in northern Michigan.

The wood-panel walls and the musty smell of my father's house remind me of my youth. Little has changed here, except now a hospital bed sits in the middle of the living room with Dad lying unconscious on top of it.

How could my consciousness of the moments between talking to him on the phone and traveling here have evaporated? How long have I even been here? It doesn't feel like long, but he was able to talk over the phone then and now he can't utter a single word. He lies here like the breathing dead.

People don't travel from one place to another with no knowledge of the journey. There must be some clue that I've missed. Something must have happened in the last few days that turned into this mental break from reality, or whatever this is. I sit back and think hard to recall the details of the last few days before everything changed...

2 Days Before...

Monday had started like most other mornings of my adult life. My alarm clock rang at 6:00 a.m. Five minutes later, I pulled the cranky shower knob, and when the water turned warm, I began my seven minutes of scrubbing. When my phone alarm chimed, I got out and dried off, combed my long, blonde hair, and dressed in the next outfit in my ten-day clothing rotation. I poured water into the bowl of instant oatmeal and set it in the microwave for twenty-five seconds. When I was done, I sat down, listened to the morning news, and ate.

My gaze wandered around the kitchen and then over to the living room. My apartment had changed so little over the eight years that I'd lived there. It made me happy. People were so quick to change things unnecessarily. When I finished watching the news, I left the TV on since it made good company. My mornings, like most parts of each day, were well organized. Removing the unexpected kept the stress down. That was what I'd learned in life.

Unwashed dishes were intolerable, so I scrubbed my bowl and cup and then opened a can of food for Fluffers. He rubbed on my leg, as usual, until I forked the cat food into his bowl. Then he ate with enthusiasm, like he'd never eaten before, exactly like he does every time. Cats are so much more predictable than people. Maybe that's why I preferred their company. On Saturdays, I volunteered at the animal shelter. I pet the cats and played with them so they're friendly and get adopted. They were my closest friends.

When my kitchen chores were done, I went into the bathroom to finish getting ready. I hated looking in the mirror, but I forced myself to as I blow-dried my hair nice and straight like I always did. I applied light cover-up, mascara, and a clear gloss. That was the extent of my beauty preparations. My Aunt May told me years ago that I should spend time cultivating my beauty, that I had nat- ural beauty like my mother did, but even if that were true, I wouldn't want the attention.

The clock on my phone read 7:20 a.m., so I walked out of my apartment on time as usual. The late winter wind blew hard that morning as I trekked two blocks down Third Street. I walked the same blocks to work every day. I liked to find the most efficient way to get somewhere and not alter it. Some people took different ways through the Chicago blocks for fun. I'd never understood that.

I crossed left on Maple Street, walked straight two blocks, and turned right onto Hill Road at Café Bean, where I sometimes stopped when I felt tired or reckless. Five more blocks down Hill Road and then I reached the office of Douglass Accounting.

Accounting was the perfect job for me—low on people and high on numbers. It's a profession that often gets mis- represented as boring. Dealing with people's complaints and mood swings all day long would be boring. Lucky for me, I didn't have to do that. Most of the conversations be- tween workmates were voluntary, so I did my best to avoid them. I did have to talk to clients on occasion, but they usually weren't interested in small talk. They wanted to talk numbers which was my kind of language. It may sound strange, but I'd always loved numbers. Numbers were honest. They contained no mystery, no nuance. They were reliable in ways people could never hope to be.

My early arrival gave me fifteen minutes to situate myself at my cubicle. I sat down with a steaming cup of slightly bitter coffee and looked around, as I usually did, before the others arrived. Many of my co-workers decorated their tan cubicles with pictures, their children's artwork, or fake plants. No matter how many times I tried, I couldn't understand this waste of energy. It wasn't home, so why pretend? I kept my cubicle organized. Besides my computer, I had small plastic cubes that hold all my needed materials and a company calendar attached to the wall.

At 8:00 a.m., I promptly started to work, immersing myself in the numbers. The sounds and movements in the office disappeared from my mind when I worked. I existed in a quiet peaceful work bubble. Sometimes I'd be surprised when co-workers started to leave for lunch. Monday had been that kind of day, where the numbers filled my mind, and time moved quickly.

Tommy Gilfin showed up at my desk at lunchtime, as he often did. His last name reminded me of an elf for some reason, but Tommy looked nothing like an elf at a towering 6'2". He stood slightly stooped while he leaned against my cubicle wall. Something about his grin was slightly goofy but in a good way that made me want to smile back. I resist though, because I didn't want to encourage him. Yet, I had to admit his eyes were the warmest brown I'd ever seen. If I were to ever allow myself to like anyone, I might concede to Tommy's advances, despite his use of a nickname fit for a boy.

About six months ago, I'd given Tommy the sliver of hope which fueled his persistence. It reminded me that losing control caused nothing but regret. We both attended a party to celebrate the retirement of one of the other accountants. In general, I avoided parties and social gatherings, but the owner of our firm insisted that everyone attend. It coincided with my birthday, although I didn't tell anyone. I didn't usually mind loneliness, but that day it welled up inside me. Conversation with Tommy was warm and welcoming, and the drinks—also something I usually avoided—went down fast. We sat out on the patio of the restaurant long after the rest of the Douglas staff had left. I can't remember what we talked about, but it felt so good to talk and laugh with Tommy. Before I could stop him, he leaned over and kissed me. Before long, we were at his apartment, clothes crumpled on the floor. He mumbled about how he had liked me for so long and had dreamed of being with me.

I don't like to think about that night, but not because it had been bad. In between the tangle of drunken, uncoordinated limbs, something sweet passed between us. I didn't know how sex usually felt since Tommy was the only second person I'd slept with in my twenty-five years. I shouldn't even count the first—a college classmate who seemed not only inexperienced but bad at the whole thing. It might seem strange to only have been with two people by my age, but I don't really do relationships.

For a brief moment, when Tommy was inside me, I felt some kind of spark of feeling that I'd never had before. I wished, for that moment, that I could be different. But I couldn't. When he finished, my joy clouded over with something dark. I couldn't catch my breath. Anxiety welled in me. It made my heart drum even faster. My mind screamed to stay away from the kind of feelings I wanted to have for Tommy. Those feelings were dangerous. I knew that other people handed their hearts out recklessly. I couldn't do it even if I wanted to. I put my clothes on and told Tommy that our encounter had been a mistake, and he had to forget it.

At first, Tommy seemed hurt and tried to convince me that we should give things a try, maybe go on a few dates. That showed how little he knew about me because I'd never been one to change my mind. Eventually, he'd conceded. He said that he understood my perspective, though I doubt he really did. He also said it was okay, but based on his persistence, clearly it was not. It was just another example of how people never were what they said they were. People can't be trusted. He told me that we could be friends. Even though I found his tenacity annoying, there was something about his eyes that keep me from completely severing our tie. Anyway, he was the only friend on earth that I had, unless you counted cats.

Tommy stood in front of me and asked what he often asked me: "So, Amy Clark, are you going to get some lunch with me today?"

I sighed. I had heard this question many times. "Not today. I've got too much work to do. I think I'll stay and eat while I work."

"Are you sure you couldn't use a break? Those numbers can give you a headache after a while." He nodded, eyebrows raised.

"Maybe another time. Thanks for asking," I said, and turned back to my work.

"Okay. I'll ask again tomorrow. Maybe you'll change your mind."

I couldn't shoot him down forcefully. He seemed so hopeful and somehow I didn't want to take that away from him. After all, he was a nice guy. I just had no interest in dating. Too risky. "Enjoy your lunch," I told him.

Out of the thirty employees that worked on our floor, only Tommy acknowledged my existence. Sure, some of the others had tried to talk to me, but I had the habit of shutting the door of goodwill to anyone who opened it. I didn't even try, it just happened naturally. People usually gave up. They probably assumed that I was a snob or a bitch. I didn't think I was either, but I definitely didn't do well with people.

1 Day Before…

Tuesday began much like Monday had, then at lunch things went sour. I walked next door to buy a sandwich and when I came back to my cubicle there was a long decorative box on my desk. In it were a dozen pink roses. They smelled putridly sweet. Before I read the card, I knew they were from Tommy. Who else would send me roses? It irritated me to no end. How dare he move things past the level of playful flirting—if you could even call it that– to where I had to turn him down irrevocably? Now I'd be friendless. Again. I decided to do what I usually did in stressful situations: move on with my routine. I put the flowers on the floor on the far side of my cubicle and ignored them while I immersed myself in my reliable numbers.

At lunch Tommy came to my desk, cheeks blushing. "Did you like your gift?"

I hated to squash Tommy's spirit, but the time had come to set him straight. I didn't want a relationship with him, or anyone. Ever. He should move on and find a nice girl. I was not one of those girls. "Thank you for the flowers, but please don't do that again."

His face drooped with disappointment, the pink from his cheeks changed to white, and his puppy dog eyes looked down. "I was just trying to do something nice for you. That's all."

"I don't mean to be rude, but don't buy me anything like that again. We can be friends, Tommy, but that's all."

His tall stature seemed to shrink. "Who said we were anything but that?" Then he walked away.

Tommy ruined numbers for me on that day. My annoyance with him spoiled my focus. The sounds of my coworkers, their movements, and occasional coughs distracted me. By the end of the workday, I felt like a carbonated bottle that had been violently shaken and capped tight.

On my way home from work, I decided to stop by Café Bean for some decaffeinated coffee and something chocolaty. I hoped that the rare indulgence would soothe my frustration. Before ordering, I went into the bathroom and threw away the pink roses; their petals looked bright against the garbage-bag plastic and used paper towels.

Normally I would have enjoyed a purchased treat at home and not risked the scrutiny of others by eating in public, but that day I broke some rules. The slushy snow and cold made me want to snuggle indoors, even if it wasn't home. I'd finally started to relax, chewing my chocolaty brownie, when my phone rang. It startled me because no one called my cell phone except for my dad. His number lit up the screen, but I decided not to answer it. Moments later, the phone beeped with a voicemail.

Something gnawed at my mind. My dad rarely called me. I decided to listen to the voicemail.

"Hello?" He worked a moment to clear his throat. "This is your father. I have… some news, so give me a call. Soon. Thanks."

I'd never heard my father use those words: "I have news." Something was up. I chewed the last of the brownie, its sugariness deflated by the impending conversation with my father. His sporadic calls disrupted my habit of not thinking of him at all.

I walked out of the café and made the call. I walked down Hill Road as I listened to the phone ring.

Father answered, his voice groggy. "Hello?"

"Hello, it's Amy." I never said "me." I'd overheard people say, "It's me," but I worried that he would ask, "Who?" I guess you could say we weren't close.

"Hi." He paused, and I heard rustling in the background. "I…I…" I had never heard him wobble with his words like that before. He didn't generally talk much, but when he did, he had a sure and concise way of speaking.

Even when my mom had died, he didn't have much to say, but he didn't falter with his words.

He continued, "I guess it's best to be direct here." He breathed deeply into the phone. "I went to the doctor, and it turns out I have cancer."

I crossed onto Maple Road and followed pedestrians without looking up at the crossing sign or cars. "Cancer?" The word left a foul taste in my mouth.

"Yes. Pancreatic. I guess it's fatal. I've known for a while now, but I'm calling you because…well, I need you to come home."

I pictured my apartment and wondered if he was there. I watched the slush squish around my boots as I walked on the sidewalk. Words swam around my head, but I couldn't make them coagulate into sensible sentences.

Father continued, "I… I don't have long is what they say."

I neared the corner of Maple and Second Street. "I'm sorry. I don't know what to say."

"Will you come back to Michigan? Do you think you can get some time off work?" He never pleaded with me for anything; mostly he ignored me. This was not the father I knew.

Tears welled up and dropped down onto my wet boots. One left a tiny clean spot in the muddy slush there. I was amazed by the power of my tear. I watched it, mesmerized, as my foot stepped down from the sidewalk onto the blacktop of the road.

"Of course I—"

That is the last thing I remember before traveling from Chicago to Roscommon, Michigan.

{2}

Hearing Things

Despite replaying the days before my blackout, I'm not any closer to solving my dilemma. I still have no idea how I got here. It seems like I haven't been here long. I only remember being here today, but I don't know. The only thing I know with certainty is that my dad is dying.

For all these years, some part of me has maintained the childish view that he is invincible. His hard, stoic nature had always seemed so strong that I thought it could keep anything out—even death.

The house looks the same. The pine-paneled living room walls look more like they belong in a cabin than a house. I look everywhere but at Father in front of me: the sagging bookshelves crammed with books, the WWII memorabilia, and boxes lying around, bulging with stuff. Yet all the disorder of his house fails to take my mind from the motionless man lying in the bed. He has not moved or uttered a word since I arrived. If I couldn't see his chest moving as he breathes, I would think he was dead.

Rhonda, the nurse, assures me that he's alive. She's been here since I arrived, whenever that was. I would ask her how or when I arrived, but I can't figure how to do that without sounding insane.

I have yet to see Rhonda's face. She wears a surgical mask that covers her nose and mouth. I find it irritating. I can't help staring at it as she comes to check on Father.

"Why do you wear that mask?" I ask her.

"I've been fighting something and I would hate to pass it along."

"Do you really think it matters at this point?"

"That's not for me to decide. So for now, I'll wear the mask."

"Can he feel anything? Can he even hear us right now?"

"I don't know if he can feel anything. Hearing your voice will likely soothe him though. He may or may not understand what you're saying, but you should keep talking to him anyway. It could help you both."

"Okay, I'll try, but I've got to admit, it seems a bit strange."

"Lots of things are strange, but it doesn't make them any less true."

She squints at me. I can't tell if it's because she's smiling or thinking. Her eyes are a stunning blue.

"Alright, I'll give it a try."

"Well, I'm off. I'll be back soon. He's all set for now."

"Bye. And thanks."

I watch Rhonda walk away.

Impending death should bring sadness, not internal conflict. Yet, that is what I'm dealing with. Of course I'm sorry for Dad to have to go through pain and the fear of the unknown. If I believed in prayer, I would pray for him. Yet, if I'm honest with myself—and this is painful to even think—I will be relieved when this part of my life is over. Unpleasant things are best not thought about, and when he's gone it will be easier not to think about him. Long ago, his heart went cold toward me, and mine in turn did the same.

This is too much to think about, so I look for distraction. The television hasn't been updated in decades, but I can't remember how to operate it.

"In this day and age, you must be the only person without cable, Dad. How do you stand it?"

My question hangs in the air, unanswered.

The television crackles with static when I switch it on. I turn the ancient knobs, trying to find some morning news. Then I could make oatmeal, or some kind of breakfast, and try to regain at least some of my routine. The television refuses to cooperate. I gently turn the knob until the fuzziness gives way to a grainy picture. Two middle-aged women look at a young woman modeling an outfit. It's not what I had in mind, but it will do, except that it is mute. I slowly turn the sound knob yet I hear nothing.

A static charge begins to creep up my arm, raising the hair along with it. I worry that I'm being electrocuted by the ancient television. I try to let go of the knob but can't. An unseen force holds my arm in place. The television starts to vibrate, along with my arm, then my body. A booming sound bursts in my ears. I want to cover them, but only one hand is free. I use that hand and my shoulder and protect my ears.

The sound grows louder. It becomes a deep, booming voice. A male voice. It comes from the television, from the room, from inside my head.

"YYOOUU SEEEEEE."

I jump backward, away from the set. My arm is free. I land on the floor and see the same two women on the screen. Now I hear their voices. The booming voice, the vibration, the electricity, are all gone. Were they ever there? They couldn't have been. I lay there for a minute, waiting for my heart's rhythm to return to normal.

I turn to look at my dad. He appears unfazed. "I got a good zap from that old thing. That's dangerous, Dad. It could have killed me! You should take care of that." I realize the futility of my words. I cross my arms over my chest to stop them from shaking.

The morning news continues for thirty more minutes. I stare at it with no interest and little comprehension, at a loss for what to do next. I'm trying not to think of how scared that shock had made me.

The program changes to a morning talk show. I realize that sitting is making me even more anxious. I am not a sit-around type of person. Time is meant to be filled. I miss my routines. I miss my reliable, safe numbers. I've got to do something.

I move to turn the television off when I realize two things. One, I am not touching that television with my bare hands ever again. Two, the cat on the commercial makes me realize that Fluffers has no one to feed him. I have no idea where my phone is so I use Dad's old school corded phone. Sadly, I have my super's number memorized because I've called him so many times to repair the ridiculous amount of things that break in my apartment. His voicemail recording sounds strange, like I'm hearing it through a tunnel or something. I leave a detailed message asking him to hire the pet service that comes to our building and give them a copy of my key. I also tell him the only kind of food that is acceptable for Fluffers, how often he needs to be played with, and to have the pet service call my Father's number to report and get my credit card information. Poor Fluffers. I miss him already.

I turn the TV off with pliers that have rubber-coated handles, just in case. I wander around Dad's large living room. The same pictures hung on these walls when I was a child. They probably weren't as dusty then. This place hasn't been dusted in weeks, maybe longer. Large book shelves stand along two of the walls. Some of the shelves are crammed with books facing all directions, other shelves are covered with WWII memorabilia stacked on top of more memorabilia, and a few are covered with items that could only have come from television infomercials. Overflowing cardboard boxes sit on the floor in front of the bookshelves. It looks like their contents want to escape. Everything in the room is covered with dismal dust.

The disorganization and dankness call to me, and now I have a job to pass the time. I search the kitchen cabinets until I find suitable cleaning supplies—rolls of paper towel and garbage bags. I stand on a chair to reach the top of a bookshelf and start there. Clouds of dust float down from my work. I'm the one who needs a mask. I start stacking books in piles on the floor. "Sorry to get rid of these, Dad, but you probably won't need them anymore. Don't you want someone else to enjoy them? I won't get rid of your favorites." Although I don't have a clue what those would be, I want to reassure him if he can hear. Eventually, I will have to go through all the things in this house, so why not get it over with?

On the next shelf, I find a picture of my parents. They are young and have their arms wrapped around each other, smiling blissfully, unaware of a future child or impending death. I haven't looked closely at a picture of my mother in years. How is it that we look similar, but she is beautiful? It must be the tweak of a few small angles that separate beauty from ugliness. I could never be pretty like her. Maybe it's her joy. I don't feel particularly happy, but it looks like she was. Does anyone feel happy like that for more than a brief moment? My hands begin to shake. It must be from the work of cleaning. My eyes start to well up against the dust. I put the photo down and continue my battle against the dust.

The pile of books and things to donate is growing and the shelves grow bare. I go through three more shelves before I run across another picture. It is lying face down underneath a pile of books. It's strange to look at a picture of your young self and remember the exact emotion you felt when someone snapped the photo. A smile rested on my young lips, but I recognize those unhappy eyes—the eyes of my youth.

It was the beginning of what I think of as "the forgetting." That year my dad had slowly begun to forget about me. His neglect grew and continued until I was the rare, obligatory phone call that he made to another state and didn't seem to enjoy. This picture was taken on my eighth Christmas. The previous Christmas, I hadn't expected much in terms of gifts. I didn't even think much about them since it had only been forty days since Mother's death. But my eighth Christmas, I'd hoped for some joy. I *needed* it. I left Santa-dad a list weeks ahead of time so there would be no guesswork for him. Dad didn't buy one thing on my list though. Not one thing! It looked as if he had bought toys for some other little girl—dolls and nail polish when I'd asked for books and science kits. I never played with dolls. Even worse than the toys was the strange fake, plastic smile he wore most of the morning. He'd seemed to look through me, as if I were transparent. It was a look that I would come to know well over the years. After I opened my gifts that morning, he took my picture—this picture—before sitting down to read a WWII book he'd bought himself. Besides eating—which of course was frozen and canned food (that was all we ate after Mother's death)—that was the extent of our interaction that day.

I'd hoped that it would be a one-time thing, but after he forgot my birthday the following March and generally forgot about everything else to do with me, I realized that things were not going to change. I became invisible to him. He barely acknowledged my existence. On the rare moments when he asked me a question, I gave a reassuring smile with a short answer and then went on with my own thing. Faking my emotions this way was what made life tolerable.

I put the photo face down and continue to replace dirty disorganization with clean, bare, order.

***

Hours later, Rhonda opens the door, apparently past the point of knocking to announce herself. I've been so busy that I hadn't noticed how much time had passed. The sun sinks low in the late winter sky while I sit back in one of Father's leather chairs. My stomach growls for attention, but I'm too exhausted to move.

Rhonda looks around the room, mask moving as she asks, "Been busy?"

Something about this woman appeals to me, so I smile. "Yes, I had some time, and it needed to be done."

"Well I'm sure Harold will appreciate it."

For a moment I blank out, I don't hear Father's first name often. "Yea, I'm sure."

Rhonda walks over and performs some checks on my dad's equipment. "Have you been talking to your father?" Rhonda asks.

"No. I don't know what to say." My cheeks burn from the small lie. I can't admit that I *had* been talking to him, although I'm not sure why.

"It's not necessarily *what* you talk about, more just the sound of your voice," Rhonda reminds me. "Give it a try. It will comfort him. It might even do you some good."

"I don't know. Maybe I'll try."

"Have you eaten yet? I noticed there's only soup and other canned goods in the pantry. You might have to go into town tomorrow to get some supplies. Do you know how long you're staying?"

"I haven't really thought about that. I don't even know how I got here, to be honest." I laugh at my slip, hoping that she won't take it seriously.

"These things are stressful. You might not feel like yourself. It's normal."

"Do you know how long...?" I don't know how to phrase the question without sounding like a jerk.

"There is no definite schedule to these things. It could be days or weeks. The important thing is that we keep him comfortable. You do your part, and I'll do mine."

"Okay. Well, I left a message for my boss and said I would be out for about two weeks. I'm sure I could get more time if I need it. I never take time off, so..."

"Whatever you can give is good." Rhonda winks at me. "Why don't you get some food and rest while I'm here?"

"Thanks."

I have no idea how long I've been here or exactly how long I will stay. What is the protocol for these things? Dad asked me to come, but I can't stay indefinitely. What would I even do here for one week—besides go crazy? I decide to keep myself busy for the week getting his house in order, and then I'll think about week number two.

I heat up a can of soup and eat it gratefully, despite the sour taste it leaves in my mouth. My whole childhood consisted of canned food and microwavable fare. I still eat frozen food, but I hate the canned stuff. Tomorrow, I'll have to go to town. I crave fresher food.

This room is overwhelming me with its piles of dust and my unmoving father. I decide take a break from it and rest in the spare room. It looks like he didn't dust or clean in here for a long time either, so I'll have to put that next on my to-do list. I find an old Steinbeck book on a shelf and lay back on the comforter to read it. One of the only things I have in common with my dad is a love of books.

In my actual life, I prefer predictability and no adventure, but I love how in fiction you can have perilous journeys, lurid love affairs, friends, laughter, tears—a life—but a safe life that doesn't involve the real heartache that comes from real relationships. In real life there are no happy endings.

***

I'm startled awake and open my eyes to darkness. When did I fall asleep? Why is my heart racing like I just missed death? A heavy weight pushes down against my chest. I take deep breaths and try to regain a normal cardiac rhythm. I didn't have a bad dream, so why is my heart thumping, and how did I fall into such a deep sleep so early in the evening?

A booming voice shatters the silence. "YOU SEEEE; I SEEEE."

I fly out of bed. The voice surrounds me and is inside me like the voice from the TV. It bellows next to me in the dark. My fists instinctively rise.

"What?" I yell, turning my body to face the unseen threat. "Who's there?" I scream.

I hear the furnace humming down the hall in its attempt to heat the house. I jump again before I recognize the sound. I stumble as I run to the light switch and slam it up. The room is empty. The only movement is my shaking hands. I force myself to run down the hallway and switch on every light in my path on my way to Father's room. The gun cupboard door squeaks as I open it. These guns might be loaded or empty, but either way, the fierce look of a shotgun will scare—or serve as a bludgeon if nothing else.

"You'd better run! I'm going to shoot you if I see you!" I yell as I run out of the bedroom and into the living room.

Lights illuminate the house but show no sign of any intruder. Father lies quiet and unconscious, his color tinged with green in the light of night. I turn on every outside light and look around. Nothing is out of place: no doors are open, no footprints dent the fresh snow, no evidence that anyone else is awake but me.

Inhaling deeply, I sit down in the living room with my dad.

"Did you hear that, Dad?" I find the irony of the question kind of funny, but I'm too frightened to laugh. "Of course you didn't. You're lucky, because that was fucked up. Excuse my language, but that's the only way to describe it. If you weren't already near death, you might be after that. I feel like I am."

The sound of my rapid breath and hammering heart fill my ears. My hands and feet tingle as the blood slowly returns to the rest of my body. All I can do is breathe, slow and deep, until my body calms down. I wish I had a habit that calmed me, like smoking or something. The shotgun rests against my body as I lean back in Father's leather chair.

My adrenaline finally subsides and my body feels exhausted and twitchy. With each breath, my body relaxes a little more. If I weren't so terrified, I would fall asleep. The quiet surrounds me. I fight the sagging of my eyelids.

I realize I'm nearly asleep when I hear the voice again, softer, but deep. "YOU SEEEE; I SEEEE," it says.

"Ahhhh!" For a quick moment, I think the voice screaming is someone other than me, and then I realize that it *is* me, but I sound strange and strained. I yell until my voice cracks. "Leave me ALONE!!"

I clench the cold shotgun tightly as I run through the house, pointing my protection behind every door, under every bed, and inside every closet. Then I look out all the windows and check for footprints in the snow. I jerk the front door open. The floodlights near the porch clash against the night. "LEAVE ME ALONE!" I scream into the darkness.

My body slumps into a living room chair. "I'm going crazy, Dad."

I stand and lay the shotgun across a table. Carrying it is pointless. "When people hear voices, it means only one thing. They are losing it. This is bullshit. I just can't believe it. It's messed up." I watch my aimless feet pace the living room floor, listen to squeaking floorboards.

My eyes pace the room too, and I notice Father's sad excuse for a liquor cabinet. It's really a buffet table that he thought hid his liquor. When I open the cabinet door, light glints off the bottles inside. Dad never drank himself to oblivion in my presence, but he enjoyed a glass of whiskey on many nights. I remember the smell of it on his breath.

It can't make things much worse, although I'm not much of a drinker. The whiskey pours out golden brown. Maybe it won't be so bad. I tip back the glass and gulp it down, spitting and spewing some across the room.

"Oh my... How can you drink this? It tastes awful!" Despite the gag reflex, I force more down. I can't seem to sit, so I walk the room and drink. It burns my throat. Soon the alcohol tingles through my veins. In college, I didn't consume alcohol like most students. I liked to be in control. The tingling reminds me of the night with Tommy when I let myself go and drank too much. Would I have had sex with him if I were sober? Absolutely not.

I lose track of time. The alcohol numbs my body and helps loosen the fear from my mind.

"I don't usually like to talk, but you look like you could use some conversation," I say to my quiet father. My drink almost spills when I sit down. "It's not fair, you know. I shouldn't go crazy. I've had my fill of bad luck. Lost Mom. You weren't a picnic to deal with. No offense." I feel a little lightheaded and lean over the side of the chair. "I just wanted to get through life with no more major stuff. A straightjacket means major stuff. Doesn't it?" The image of padded walls comes to mind. "You know what? You're a much better listener now." Laughter bursts out of me, and I sit back.

***

Consciousness announces itself slowly. I must have slept. Something beeps persistently in the background. The sun wants to boil my eyelids. I open my eyes and they scream in pain. "Oh. Oh my gosh," I say to no one. I cradle my hot forehead with my cold hands.

"Here," a voice says, making me jump. I thought I was hearing "those" voices again, but this was a real one, with a hand reaching toward me. Rhonda moves closer. "Looks like you could use these." she places two white pills and a glass of water on the table beside me. "Rough night?"

Rhonda questions as she waves her hand toward the whiskey bottle. She carries the empty glass away.

"Ah." I try to adjust my scrunched, aching limbs to grab for the pills. "Yeah, I guess it was. Thanks."

"Do you want to talk about it?" Rhonda asks.

"No, I'm good. Just wanted a drink, that's all."

"Okay. Why don't you go rest? I'll clean this up and care for your father."

My body is stiff and still drunk. Wordlessly, I drag myself from the living room to the guestroom and plop onto the bed, coverless, and pass out within minutes.

***

Before I open my eyes, I hear that soft beeping again—an internal metronome. What is it? Probably the sound of the tumor or cancer in my brain ticking away the minutes until it wins the game. Or maybe it's part of my insanity.

The clock reads 2:12 p.m. in red numbers. I will my body out of bed and amble to the bathroom. I sit there longer than I need to. I am lost without my schedule. If I had that, at least I would have something to will away the time before I'm stone cold crazy or dead.

Movement is all that will keep these panicked thoughts at bay. I check on my dad. He's lying in bed, motionless, breathing heavy. Nothing new there. I don't see Rhonda or anyone else. I invite some television company—using the coated pliers—pop some more painkillers, and drink lots of water. The cupboards are fairly bare, but I scrounge to find a can of mandarin oranges and eat them.

This lack of routine is making my skin crawl. The air is heavy with boredom. Anxiety starts to fill my brain and thoughts about the previous night begin to push in. "Dad, I need some air. Do you need anything? No? Okay, if I don't come back in an hour, tell Rhonda that a bear woke and had me as a late-winter snack."

My boots sit by the door, waiting for me. How can they be there when I don't remember packing them? I put my coat, hat, and gloves on—all of which have materialized from who knows where—and head out the door.

The forest surrounding Father's house is like an old friend. As a girl, I spent most of my free time exploring and claiming the woods, all twenty-five acres of them. Even in the winters of endless snow I would throw on snowshoes and traverse the land. Now, all the winter snow is beginning the great melt. The crisp air is invigorating as I walk through the slushy snow to my favorite place on the property.

In some spots where the sun hasn't reached, the snow crunches under my feet. I move toward the stream, which shimmers in the light. The water seems higher than when I last saw it, but that was years ago. This stream was my closest childhood friend. Really, my only friend—I wasn't any better as a child at making friends. The stream helped me escape Father's inattentions. It rarely disappointed me. The sound of its trickling waters calmed my nerves. On warm days, I brought books with me and vicariously adventured with all kinds of characters. An old fallen tree had provided a place to sit in those days; now a new fallen tree took its place acting as a makeshift bench.

I sit down and listen to my old friend babble in the language of water. I listen to the birds, who chatter throughout the woods looking for rendezvous. I'd forgotten how much I love these sounds. The horrid events of the night seep out of my mind, and for the first moment since my arrival, I feel truly relaxed.

The sun warms my face and soothes me. The peace lasts until I notice a moment later that my toes are going numb. I need to get my blood pumping. It's time to move.

I decide to explore the old paths that cross the property. As a girl, I knew most of the forest paths, which were created by animals, shade, or my own tireless feet. It's hard to see the paths now with the different degrees of snow-melt, but it seems to me that they have changed. My legs begin to ache from battling the snow, but I push on.

The only thing I miss about this place is the land. It was always so easy to find the solitude that I craved here. It's harder to avoid people in Chicago, but there is a kind of public aloneness that is possible.

My legs burn and threaten to give out on me. The snow crunches with each step back to the stream. I find the new resting log and rub my sore thighs. The birds chatter the same as when I left. I hear a commotion of scratching and scraping and see two squirrels fighting over territory nearby. They chase each other right onto the log where I sit. One looks at me and runs away. The other chirps at me with its tail fluffed out over its head. It looks almost defiant.

"What are you doing little guy?" I ask in my talking-to-my-cat-Fluffers voice.

The squirrel moves toward me, making strange hiss-like sounds. The sound changes. "Ch, ch, ch," it chants.

"Are you a deranged little squirrel?" I continue in my sing-song voice. "I don't need any more problems, like a bite from a rabid or virus-ridden rodent." I slowly stand. "You stay right there, and I'll leave." I move with deliberate caution and keep looking behind me to make sure it doesn't pounce on my head or anything. The sound that the squirrel is making changes again. "S, s, s," it sounds like. When I look back, the squirrel is at the edge of the log closest to me. Its tail is no longer puffed out. Now it stands on its hind legs, waving its paws in my direction, staring at me. "Sssee, sssee, see," the squirrel jabbers.

"Shut up squirrel!" I kick a pile of snow at it.

"See, ch, see," it continues.

"I'm going to get you, you little—" I stumble over into the crusty snow. My hands slam in the coldness, and I jump up, determined to wring that squirrel's neck. The squirrel scampers up an oak tree and takes up its call again.

"Shut up!" I gather a snowball to throw at it, but it's not heavy enough to make the distance. I dig deeper and find a rock but it misses the squirrel. My hands dig into the slush. The wetness seeps through my gloves, but I find more rocks. No matter how hard I throw them, they don't come close to the squirrel. It sits on its branch mocking me.

"Ahh, fuck you squirrel!" I yell and turn away before I'm tempted to climb that tree. I'd never had an urge to kill something before.

I hear it behind me while I trudge as fast as I can toward Father's house. "See, see," it calls.

***

I walk into the house, wiping the sweat off my face, catching my breath, wondering whether that squirrel is the hallucination of a psychotic person or the result of a disease snaking through my brain. My thought is cut short by the aroma of simmering sauce and cooking meat. It smells good. Rhonda is in the kitchen stirring something in a pot.

Her back is facing me when she says, "I hope you don't mind, I brought some food for you. You must be tired of canned meals. You might want to go into town later or tomorrow and stock up for your stay."

"Thanks. It smells delicious." My brain feels like it's been through the blender. I don't know how to feel between the psycho squirrel and the smell of actual food, which makes my mouth water.

Rhonda turns around. Is that a startled look in her eyes? "Are you all right? You look like you've seen a ghost," she says through her mask.

Why doesn't she take that damn mask off? "I'll be fine. I'm just tired from my walk."

"Get some rest then and eat. Your father's all set on his pain meds, I changed the catheter. Everything looks fine. The night nurse will be along later to check on things."

"The night nurse? Was there a night nurse last night? I didn't see anyone."

"Oh, they are crafty like that. They know how to slide in and out quietly so as not to wake anyone. I'm sure they were here."

Maybe that can explain something about the sounds I heard. Actually, I doubt it since there was the squirrel too.

Rhonda stares at me for a moment too long. "Are you sure everything is okay?"

"I think I'm just hungry." On cue, my stomach growls.

"This should take care of that," she says, pointing at the pot of food. "I'll see you tomorrow, then. Don't worry; things will get better. You see."

"What did you just say?" My jaw tightens.

"I said things will get better. You'll see."

I stare at Rhonda, trying to determine if she is real or not. She looks real enough, but did I hear her right? It must be me. She squints, and I think she is giving me that I-feel-sorry-for-you smile. She turns to gather her things.

After Rhonda leaves, I stand motionless for some time, unsure of what my next step should be. I guess even if you're hearing things, you still need to eat, so I fill a bowl with chili and sit down in the leather recliner next to Father.

"Well, Dad, everything looks pretty much the same around here. I wish I could say the same for myself, but you see, I am going crazy."

Chewing the chili lightens my mood briefly. It's been a long time since I've eaten anything good.

"How do I know I'm going crazy, you might ask? Well, let me explain. I'm hearing things. Booming voices in the night, talking squirrels, that kind of shit. I don't know what it means, but it's just crazy. I don't know what to do.

It's not like they give you a manual for this sort of thing. I wish I had someone to talk to. No offense to you, but let's face it, you never were a good listener. At least, not with me."

Father's response is calm, consistent breaths.

{3}

Seeing Things

"I hope you don't mind, but I think I'll sleep here in this chair, Dad. Sleeping in the guestroom seems like an invitation for disaster. Not that you can protect me, but it's better than being alone. The night nurse will probably wake me and scare the crap out of me, but at least that's someone real."

I find an afghan, one I remember from my childhood. I can't picture my mother's face or remember what her voice sounds like, but I can remember her covering me up in this afghan on cold nights. It smells somewhat musty, like everything else in this house, but it's soft and reminds me of my mom, so I wrap myself in it tightly.

"I think I'll leave the light on tonight. Is that okay with you?"

Father remains unmoved.

"I'll take that as a yes."

I lay back and close my eyes, listening to the sounds of the house: the hum of the furnace, Father's breathing, and an occasional annoying beep. I pull the blanket up under my chin.

The arrival of morning surprises me. After all the craziness of yesterday, I'm surprised that I fell asleep so quickly again. I guess insanity makes me sleepy. I'm thankful for the sleep but stiff. Did the night nurse come? I have yet to see her. That's strange. Maybe she knows I'm crazy and wants to keep her distance.

A memory of a dream tickles my brain; a familiar voice quietly echoes from it –Tommy, from the office. I wonder how he handled my rejection. Maybe I should have been kinder to him—I kind of miss his pestering ways. No one has ever given me so much attention, except maybe my mother, and that was so long ago that it's hard to remember.

Father looks the same. "Good morning, Dad," I say rather cheerfully. "How am I, you ask? Well, it's strange, but I feel good this morning. Maybe Rhonda was right that grief can mess with your mind. Maybe yesterday was just grief baring its teeth at me."

I stand and stretch my compressed muscles. "I mean, even if we haven't talked much most of my life, I'm still sad for you, sad about you. I've read novels where grief crushes people. Maybe that's all that's going on here. Fiction probably has some truth in it, right?" I hope so.

My stomach growls with hunger. I open a can of fruit cocktail and then start making a chore list. While I'm here, I might as well make myself useful. Sitting around and drinking is doing me no good. These piles of boxes need to be sorted. The rest of this house needs to be cleaned and organized. I'll have to do it either way, eventually. Why not get it done while I'm here?

I sit back and exhale. Having a plan makes me feel better. Now I just need a list for the grocery store and my day will be perfectly planned.

***

I walk into the garage and am reminded that I still have no idea how I got to this house. There is no rental car and definitely no car service in this part of Michigan. Someone must have given me a ride to Father's house, but who? I wish that I could ask Rhonda, but I can't think of a way to sneak it into conversation without sounding unhinged.

Father's old pickup truck is familiar. I can't believe he still has his old tan Chevy. It has aged better than most people. Its old-school vinyl creaks when I climb in. I haven't driven in years, I don't need to in the city, but I'm sure it's like riding a bike. Even so, I drive slowly out of the garage and down the dirt road, which is slick with an early morning dusting of snow.

The route to town is still etched in my mind after all these years. I don't even have to think about it. I must have driven these roads hundreds of times. Dad had given me the chore of buying our canned and frozen foods as soon as I got my license.

I drive through the small town of Roscommon and realize that little has changed. There are a few more stores, fast food restaurants, and bars, but otherwise it looks the same. The old grocery store survived, a pharmacy sits beside it now. The grocery store has been expanded, but I can see the old lines that existed before. I park near the rear of the lot and head in.

Some people don't have a method for shopping. They amble aimlessly, thinking that the items they need might magically pop into their head. I have a system. It saves time, and I don't forget things. First, I always have a list. Second, I always start at the opposite side of the produce. Fruits and vegetables go in last to prevent damage. I push the squeaking cart to the far right hand side of the store. Tampons, oatmeal, milk, orange juice, and frozen meals are carefully added to the cart. I check them off the list as I go. My general social rule is no eye contact with others. Making nice only slows things down and distracts me. Some people in small towns like this one are used to saying hi or smiling at people. Despite my evasiveness, someone says hello. I miss the invisibility of the big city. I mumble hello. After that I'm more careful to look down at my cart or turn my head toward the shelves when people pass near me to prevent further interaction.

The produce aisle smells of rotisserie chicken. It must be drifting from the deli nearby. That might be a good addition when I want something besides a frozen meal. Frozen meals are the only tradition that I upheld from childhood. I break my rule of keeping my eyes pointed away from others so that I can see where to find the chicken. A man is leering at me. His eyes look hungry. I quickly turn my head away, but not before I notice how rough he looks. A shower hasn't touched the man in days or longer. His skin and hair shine with grease. Black stubble grows from his chin and cheeks in different lengths. His body is stout and muscular, like a man who works with his body. His shirt is stained and tattered. My skin crawls.

I drive my squeaking cart to the bananas, hoping to remove the sick feeling that the man caused. It feels like his eyes are burning holes in my back. What an awful person I am for being so judgmental of someone based on their appearance, but something about him disgusts me. I fill a bag with ripe bananas, my eyes cast downward while doing so, hoping to deflect any more attention from the grubby man or anyone else. I tie the bag and walk away.

From around the corner of the produce bin, a cart pushes right in front of mine. I bump it. The grimy man stands in front of me, smiling. I avoid his eyes but can't help noticing that what few teeth he has left are brown.

"Sorry. Seems we run into each other," he says with a slight slur.

I can't look at him or even talk to him. I back up and push my cart left, away from him, but he grabs it with his hand.

"What's yur name?" he asks.

"Get out of the—" I try to pull my cart away, but he's insistent and doesn't let go. I look up into his eyes. I'm seething with anger and ready to tell him where to go.

I open my mouth, but nothing comes out. His eyebrows lift in some suggestive, lewd way. I want to yell at him. I want to run away, but I am frozen. My body is paralyzed. I try to move my eyes; they hurt with the effort, but they refuse. They are focused on the man. He looks at me like he wants to devour me.

A whooshing sound grows within and outside me. It grows louder until it sounds like a tornado. I know tornado sound. When I was a young girl, Dad and I had listened to tornados brewing overhead while crouched in our basement. This sound is louder, yet it doesn't move me or create even the smallest wind. My heart rams like it will explode. My pulse runs through my veins at a rate sure to kill me. This must be the climax of my nervous breakdown. I would give anything to be able to move, to run away.

The sound bursts through my skin and ears. It hurts. Everything around me is still, frozen in time—the man, the people in the store—but I am shaking. Something is shaking me apart from within. The shaking stops. Some force starts to compress my body; it push against every part of my skin. Then I feel like I'm being pulled through a small space that I'm not fit for. My skin feels like it's stretching. It feels like it might pull apart.

This is going to kill me. I try harder to move my body, move my eyes, but all I can see is the disgusting man. What is he thinking? Is he doing this to me? I'm not sure because he is frozen too. He has a wicked sneer on his face.

Finally, I am able to blink, but when I do, his eyes look different. A light is glowing from behind them. It looks unnatural, ghoulish. The space around his eyes begins to swirl with color that swallows everything in its path, leaving a trail of darkness like a black hole. There is nothing left now but his crazed eyes. The store, the bananas, the people, are all gone.

The wind noise grows louder. I try to cover my ears from the painful sound, but my hands are no longer there. I am able to move my eyes now. I look down and see a hazy, ghostly version of myself. It is fog-like and disappearing. Where did I go?

My body is being pulled, intensely, or at least it feels like it is even though I can't see it. I feel what's left of me moving through a straight tunnel that leads into the devilish eyes of the man.

Suddenly the sound stops. I open my eyes and see that I am in a black emptiness. I try to move my arms, at least I think I'm moving them, but I can't see them. I can't touch anything, not even my own body. I have a strange sensation between my legs. Something I've never felt. There is something hanging there and it is hot. Burning hot. Hot and pleasant. What is going on? A man grunts. It sounds like a sex grunt. It must be the man. The disgusting man. I realize my eyes are shut tight. I'm not sure that I want to open them. Should I open them?

I open my eyes and see that I'm in the backseat of a car, lying on top of a half-naked woman. How can I be here? Big, hairy hands are wrapped around the woman's neck. Her face is red, veins pulse from her throat. The woman is beautiful. Beads of sweat glisten on her forehead. Her brown eyes stream tears while she glares silently at me. Me? Why am I here? I wouldn't... These are the disgusting man's hands. He is doing this to her. But why am I here?

"What's going on?" I try to scream. I hear the words in my mind, but they don't come out of my mouth. I try to move my mouth. I can't. I try to move my hands. I can't. They feel numb. They start to tingle and regain feeling. Then I realize...my fingers are wrapped around the woman's throat. I can feel the pressure of the fingers around her neck. I can feel blood pulsing through her slick skin.

I start feeling other sensations. The heat between my legs is him. Please no. Make it stop! I don't want to feel this. I try to stop him, I try to move my whole body, but nothing changes, the man continues his unwanted thrusts.

"Stop this!" I scream again and again. I can only hear it in my head. I am useless. I cannot help this poor woman.

"You are the devil! You fucking bastard! Don't kill her! Don't fucken kill her!"

The man's voice is deep, vibrating in my skull as if I had said the words. "Keep it up, and maybe I won't kill ya. You like that now, don't ya, baby," he says as he pushes into the woman.

"Ya want it harder?" He pushes deeper and faster.

The woman tries to move her head away, but the man keeps her head facing his. He jams her head further down into the stained car upholstery. The skin around her eyes stretches in her struggle to move.

I feel an intense reaction between my legs—an explosion. It must be the man's orgasm. If only I had a weapon and a way to wield it. I want to kill him.

The hands let go of the woman's neck, and he collapses on top of her. "Was it good for you, too?" he says.

The woman quakes with fear. She sobs.

The whooshing tornado sound explodes around me, and everything goes black. I open my eyes to a blinding light. I blink to defend my eyes. I look up and see that I'm standing next to the banana stand, looking at the loathsome creature who raped that woman. He eyes me expectantly.

"Get out of my way or I will kill you, you piece of shit." The words shake from my mouth. "I know what you did to the woman in the car. You belong in jail, you asshole."

His eyes grow wide, and he looks around. No one stands near us. He says nothing, but sprints toward the exit doors. He leaves behind his cart.

I have to focus on my breath. I may faint, and who knows where I'll go then. I don't want to find out. I lean over the cart and breathe. My legs feel rubbery. I lean further forward for support. I stay like this until the edges of my vision become clear and I no longer feel that threatening darkness. People are near me. An older woman gives me a sympathetic look.

"Are you alright, dear?"

I look at her. Is she real? I don't answer. I look away and move forward, pushing my cart using it like a walker.

What should I do? Should I leave the store with no food? Should I pay and go? Either way, I have to make sure that sicko doesn't follow me. Should I call the police? But what would I say? Someone was raped by someone. I don't know either one. They would ask how I know, and the truth would earn me a straitjacket.

I push the cart through the store, unsure of what to do. I pass a cashier standing in front of her lane. "Are you ready to check out?" she asks. "I'm open."

I nod and wordlessly empty my cart.

The cashier looks at my shaking hands. "Are you okay?" she says.

I nod again because I'm sure my voice is useless. I wait for her to finish ringing me through, and I pull money out of my wallet with fumbling fingers.

Tears stream down my face as the automatic doors open. The sound makes me jump. I'm sure people are watching me, but I don't care. I just want to know if the man is nearby. I scan the parking lot but don't see any signs of him. I push my cart as fast as I can to Dad's truck and shove the groceries in. Through the haze of stinging tears, I drive, watching behind me for the man.

***

I unpack the groceries in Father's kitchen. I drop frozen pasta on my foot and jump and cuss at the assault. Rhonda is watching me, but I refuse to acknowledge her. I can't. I focus all my attention on putting away the groceries. My hands still shake uncontrollably at first but finally the adrenaline starts to drain out of me. Unfortunately, so does my energy. I rub my tense forehead, drag myself to the living room, and drop into a chair.

"What's going on, Amy? What's wrong?" Rhonda furrows her eyebrows.

"Nothing," I say, my voice abnormally high. "Everything's fine."

"Clearly it's not fine. Do you want to talk about it?"

I rest my head on my hands and rub at the tension. "I'm not sure I could explain it even if I wanted to. Sorry."

"You know, grief does strange things to people. I've seen it. Whatever's going on, you will get through it. You'll see." Rhonda moves to stand next to my father.

"I don't know. I don't know that this is going to pass. Something is wrong with me."

"You're in pain. You're losing your father. It's a difficult thing—*the* most difficult thing, losing people we love."

"I haven't seen my father in years," I admit.

"That doesn't mean that you don't care."

"Doesn't it?"

"No, I don't believe it does," Rhonda reassures me.

"Have you ever heard of people…" I pause, wondering how much to divulge, "…seeing things?"

"It can happen. You can tell me about it if you'd like. I won't judge."

"I just feel like I'm losing it. I've never felt like this before." That doesn't even begin to touch on what I'm feeling, but it's all I can say.

"All I know is that these types of situations are traumatic. Don't be too hard on yourself. Whatever it is, it will get better. Maybe in the end, you'll learn something from it, although it's never easy."

"Maybe. Thanks. I think I'll go lie down for a bit. I'm exhausted."

"I see," Rhonda says, tending to my father.

I stare hard at her. Does she know what is going on? Is she toying with me? I wait for her to look my way so I can check her eyes. She returns a warm glance. The woman seems kind.

"Thanks for everything. How is my dad doing anyway?" I ask as I stand to leave.

"He's about the same. I haven't noticed any changes in him. I'll let you know if I do. I'm taking good care of him."

"I know. I appreciate that."

I leave for the spare room for the safety of solitude.

***

The squeaking door wakes me. According to the clock, I have been sleeping for hours. Rhonda is probably leaving.

I venture out of my self-imposed isolation and sit in the living room next to Father.

"It's official. Something's wrong with me," I explain to my unresponsive father. "Maybe instead of a brain aneurysm like Mom, I have a tumor, and it's making me hallucinate. Whatever it is, you're lucky you won't have to see it. Not like you saw much of anything I did anyway. I know, it's not fair. You can't defend yourself, but...it's too bad things weren't different."

I sit quietly next to my dad. Horrific visions of the woman being raped flash through my brain. I can't make them stop. They make me realize how right I am to keep people out of my life. People will only hurt you, one way or another. People kill and hurt each other every day in the name of war, power, or sex. Sometimes they do it just for kicks. The world is fucked up. All people are dangerous, some are just more obvious about it. In the end, pain is all that humans consistently give each other with their lies, violence, and abhorrent neglect. My vision grows hazy with tears.

"The world is a depressing place, Dad. You probably already know that. I guess I'd rather know that the world is evil and not be naïve like so many others. They act like the world is some happy, lollipop-filled, smiling clown circus. What bullshit. The world will eat you up if you let it. I'm not going to let it."

I stand. I have to do something. I would rather go crazy doing something than lose it while sitting around. Maybe if I keep busy it will postpone the inevitable, whatever that is.

"I'm going to sort through these boxes. You don't mind, do you?" I ask my dad.

I use the pliers to turn on the television. At least the grainy people are some sort of company.

An urgency to clean overtakes me, and I start moving with quick and decisive purpose. I hurriedly drag the garbage can and a few bags over so I can sort what should be kept and given away. The first box I rifle through is packed full of WWII memorabilia—newspaper clippings, medals, figurines.

"What was so fascinating about these things, Dad? You paid more attention to your memorabilia than to me. Someone might want this stuff, but not me. Sorry." Maybe it's worth something. I scribble *Sell* across the top of the box.

The second box I open contains all kinds of files, none of which need saving. I write *Garbage* across the top and push it next to the garbage can.

I open a third box, proud of my efficiency. The smell of lavender drifts out. The smell makes me think warmth, laughter, and hugs—my mother. When I think of her, I imagine her with a smile. It's impossible to remember the details of her face, but I remember the lift of her lips in praise of me. The house had a different feel when my mother was alive. Yes, it was clean then, but it was much more than that. It felt full of something light and airy, like the promise of spring, like love. Alone with father, it was cold, like perpetual winter.

At the top of the box rests a children's book. I don't remember my mother reading that particular book, but I do remember her reading to me. Maybe that's where my love of reading began. She read to me most nights before tucking me into bed, making sure the covers were snug, the way I liked them. I remember her talking to me as I drifted off to sleep, but I don't recall the sound of her voice.

Under the book sits a black jewelry box with fake jewels encased in rusty metal. I open the box and stare at jewelry that must have been worn by my mother. I try to imagine how she would have looked wearing each piece, but her face eludes me. I put on the necklace and slide all the bracelets onto my wrists. Somehow it makes me feel closer to her.

"Why didn't you give these to me? I had nothing of hers. It's bad enough that you would never talk about her, but you kept these things boxed up too? What good did that do?" I ask Father. "You never shared any of her life with me. You only reminded me of her death. It's almost like never having her at all."

Deeper in the box I find dried flowers, books, and a variety of small ceramic duck figurines. Did my mom like ducks? Is there a story behind that? There's so much I'll never know about her. I hold each one and try to imagine what attracted her to it. I set them aside and continue emptying the box. I find a small pillow with fine embroidery, a diary, and at the bottom of the box is a photo album. The diary feels hot in my hands. I want to read it, but I don't know if my emotions can stand anymore jolts today. I carefully set it aside.

I lay the photo album across my lap. I've seen few pictures of my mother. I carefully lift the old cover and see a young version of my mother on the first page. The black and white photo does little justice to her piercing blue eyes, but her skin looks radiant, and her smile conveys a deep happiness that I'm sure I have never experienced.

Pages and pages of her life unfold before me. Most of the people accompanying her are strangers to me. Were they family, or friends? I wish I knew something of her past, but now it's lost forever. I turn more pages and see more unknown faces. I turn another page, and there is Father. This is their life together—their wedding photo, Niagara Falls, the Mackinac Bridge, the house when they first bought it. Their smiles beam with love. I have never seen that look on my father's face. Peace and happiness rest in his eyes. Maybe he used to be different.

"What were you like before?" I ask his silent form.

On the last page of the album, there is a folded letter, dry and discolored from time.

Lu,

It's been a year since you left this good earth. I don't know why I'm writing to you. Will you hear these words? Not likely, I guess. Maybe I'm writing them to myself, to God, I don't know. I need to talk. You'd laugh at that wouldn't you? You always said I didn't talk enough.

I don't know if I can do this alone, Lu. You were the one in charge of the parenting. Maybe that wasn't right, but that's the way it was. I don't know what to do with Amy. She's a good kid, quiet like me, but good. She looks at me like she wants something, but I don't know what. I don't know what to say to her or what to do for her.

She needs a mother. Men aren't equipped to raise little girls. I'll do my best, but I worry it's not enough. You should have seen her at Christmas this year, boxes full of toys, and looks of disappointment. I don't know what went wrong.

She looks just like you. Sometimes I have trouble looking at her eyes because they remind me of you. I know that should be a good thing, but it's too hard for me. I'm not meant for much emotion, you know that better than anyone.

Anyway, I miss you. I'm putting most of your pictures and things away because I can't look at them anymore. Sorry if that makes me a bad person, but that's how it has to be. I miss you every day, and I don't need reminders.

I hope to see you someday, when my time comes. I hope there is a God and that I get to see Him. When I do, I'll have a few words to say to Him taking you away too soon.

I love you Lu,
Harold

"Bravo, Dad. You played your part at uncaring father quite well. All this time, you were just broken. Well guess what? It was hard for me, too. But you wouldn't know that because you never asked. In fact, you never asked me anything, did you? I might as well have been invisible."

I stand and make my way to the whiskey cabinet. I pour the amber liquid straight into a glass, wishing it will dull the pain, knowing it won't.

"I didn't even know that you loved her because you never said anything. Not a word. How could you do that? It was like she never existed." The liquid burns my throat, but I don't stop until the glass is empty. I pour again and pace the room. I want to break something, but instead, I pace. "Every time I asked about her you'd get so upset it felt like she died again and again for me. I just wanted to know about my mom. You could have told me things, shared her, but you didn't. You kept her life in a box. What good did that do?"

I continue my pacing, but it gets me nowhere.

"I never got into trouble at school, didn't stir the pot, stayed clean and sober, but you didn't seem to appreciate any of it." I hear my voice grow louder. "The truth is, I didn't want to see what you looked like when you were mad since you were so cold on a daily basis. Maybe I should have. Maybe it would have made things better somehow or made you see me. Who knows?"

My stomach lurches at the alcohol. I walk back and forth, trying to shake the resentment that knots in my gut. "I just don't get it. How can the man in that letter be you? If you had kindness in you, why couldn't you give it to me? I'm your daughter! I mean, I remember when I graduated—top of my class. Yes it was a small class, but still, I thought that might bring *some* emotion from you. All you did was hand me a check, and a small one at that. What the hell? Who does that? No wonder I can't stand people; I just don't get them. Everyone else's parents were nearly suffocating them with praise. My classmates seemed embarrassed by it. I was jealous. No hug, no smile. Nothing."

I stare at his silent body. I wish he could hear the words that I should have screamed long ago. "If you ever loved her, how could you treat her daughter like shit? I could count the words you said to me each month on one hand! You knew nothing about me. You didn't want to. You gave me nothing but a place to live and canned fucking food! What would mom say to *that*?"

The sound of shuffling feet interrupts my tirade. I look to see Rhonda walking towards us. "I didn't even hear you come in the door."

"I didn't know if you were sleeping, so I tried to be quiet. How's your dad doing?"

"Nonresponsive as usual."

"I'm sorry. This must be hard."

"Honestly, he's not much different now than he's been all my life."

Rhonda stares at me blankly. What must she think of me?

"What do you mean?"

"Never mind. It doesn't matter."

"It does. It might help to talk."

"Let me put it this way: he was there, but he wasn't *there*. I mean, it could have been worse, he could have abused me or something. Instead, I was nothing to him. I don't think he cared too much."

"Oh, but you're wrong there. Before he was like this, he spoke of you often. He told me how proud he was of your work in the city. He lit up when he spoke of you."

Lit up? She must be lying. Father had few emotions, and that definitely wasn't one of them. "Are we talking about the same person? That doesn't sound like him at all."

Rhonda's eyes curl up at the corners. Her mask might be hiding a smile. "He was sorry too. He told me that his greatest regret was not being a better father. There is no doubt that he loves you immensely. It sounds like he just wasn't able to show it."

It feels like a punch in the gut. Regret? "What's love if it's kept to yourself? Is that really love at all?"

"Yes, I think it is, although it is difficult to understand." Rhonda starts looking over Father's equipment. She stops and looks at me again. "May I give you some advice?"

"I guess."

"You might try forgiving your father before it's too late. Anger towards people is a heavy burden to carry, especially once they've passed."

"I'll think about it," I say, but I doubt it will happen. I wish I could forgive him, it would make things easier, but I don't know how or if he even deserves it.

Rhonda nods toward the boxes and rearranged items. "It's good that you're going through these things. Maybe you'll find some peace in the process."

"I don't know about that, but it gives me something to do."

"Speaking of something to do, I need you to do me a favor tomorrow."

"What?"

"Your father has a P.O. box in town. He got rid of his mailbox long ago because of vandals, which I'm sure you know. Anyway, could you check his mail? We can't let it get overly full."

"Sure."

"The key is on the key rack near the front door. It's marked, so you'll know which one it is. The box number is right on the key."

"Okay, I'll do that."

I watch Rhonda as she finishes her checks of my father. She moves with such tenderness.

"I think it's safe to take the mask off. I don't think you're really going to make him any sicker. And as far as I know, cancer isn't contagious."

Rhonda's eyes look like half-moons again. Why is this woman so happy? "I don't want to change the situation. Harold will go when it's his time, not any faster from my influence."

***

My fingers lay on Mother's diary, but I'm not sure that I'm ready to open it. I drink more whiskey and turn the pages. I don't want to feel any more pain today, but the curiosity moves my fingers. Maybe I will learn something about her, or somehow feel closer to her, if I read it.

3-1973

I can't believe it…I'm pregnant! I am filled with such joy! I didn't think it would happen so soon. Harold and I have been married a year. My mom warned me that it could take some time to conceive and not to get discouraged. I am over three months along. I didn't want to write about it before that because I was worried about bad luck. My pants are becoming harder to button, but I have no tell-tale bump yet. I don't think I will say anything at work until I begin to show. I will miss teaching, but Harold and I have decided that I will take some time off work until our girl (yes, I believe it must be a girl) is older.

I am going to be a mom! I still can't believe it! Harold will make a great father. He's so kind and soft hearted. I hope I'm as good of a mother as my mother was. I wish my dad was still with us so he could meet his granddaughter. I hope he is watching from heaven.

7-1973

I feel like a walking bus. I'm seven months along, but I look like full term. I am huge! I worry that Harold will find me unattractive, but his appetite for me has not changed with my size.

The baby squirms so much now. I feel her elbows and knees as she summersaults inside me. I look forward to meeting my girl. I love her already. I hope the next two months go quickly. I'm glad to be pregnant but am ready for it to be over. They don't tell you the hard sides of it, like how you feel that you could kill for food, or that you have to pee every five minutes, or how your emotions start to control you. I know all of that is only temporary. I hate to complain because I am so excited to be a mom.

10-1973

The day arrived. Amy was born on September 21st. The best day of my life (except when I met Harold). She is beautiful. I'm sure all mothers think that about their children, but she is beautiful. I look into her eyes and I feel such a strong love for her. It is different than the love I feel for Harold. It is a protective sort of love.

I'm surprised at how much work a little baby is. I no sooner feed her, burp her, and change her diaper than she needs to *be fed again. I'm told it gets easier, but tell my breasts that. They hurt! Oh well. It's a small price to pay for love.*

Harold is so gentle with her. He holds her and walks her around until she falls asleep in his arms. Sometimes, when he thinks I'm not listening, he sings softly to her. It makes me love him even more.

Who is this man my mother described? Soft hearted and singing? I wouldn't have believed it if I didn't see it written by her hand. "What happened to you?" I ask Father. He has no answer.

3-1974

I told myself that I would write more often, but it's hard to find the time. I don't want to forget these moments; I know they will go by so fast (they already have). Amy is amazing. She's 7 months old. She can sit up on her own and interact with me. I can make her laugh. What a glorious sound, her laughter. She reaches out for things but is still working to grasp and hold them tight.

I knew that I would love her, but I am sometimes overwhelmed by how emotional motherhood can be. I want to do everything right, but it's impossible. I try my best though.

Harold is such a help. I know that lots of fathers expect women to do most of the work, but he isn't like that at all. When he's at home, he focuses his efforts on her. Sometimes I have to remind him of other chores that need to be done. It's obvious, he'd rather spend his time with her. I'm a lucky woman.

I turn the page. Blank. I thumb through the rest—all blank. The last words in the diary are so false. My mother was terribly unlucky. And so am I. Life has cheated me. It may not sound horrible, but to be invisible is worse than being seen and hated. You are defenseless against it. There is no place to point the finger, except at yourself, for not being remarkable enough to be seen. I mean, how do you get an impression of yourself with a father who reflects nothing in return?

Things could have been different, but when my mother died, all hope died with her. The worst part is having no real memories of her to grasp, to feel that at one time I was loved. Father kept the memory of her away. Every time I asked him to tell me about her, give me some glimpse of the woman who surely once loved me, he would become agitated and close the conversation. Yes, Mother and I were both terribly unlucky.

I sit. Disappointment sinks in my stomach. No more words from my mother's hand, no insight into her world, just false hope. I am full of defeat. The tears fall. I curl into the chair and let them race down my checks.

***

I am awake. Or am I? I'm not sure if it's a dream. I can see very little. Blackness surrounds me like a bubble even though my eyes are open.

Unexplained sounds permeate the darkness: beeps, the fan of a heating vent, breathing. Whose breath is that? Mine?

A voice is talking, it sounds like it is reading, but I can't make out the words. I can't tell if it's male or female. It sounds like it's underwater. Whose voice is that? The voice pauses.

The sounds become clearer. "It's going to be okay," the voice says. "I love you." It burns my ears. Tommy. Tommy? Why is Tommy reading to me in my dreams and confessing his love?

***

I open my eyes. The bright morning sunshine beams through the windows and warms my skin. What a strange dream. Why was I dreaming about Tommy? Does my subconscious have a thing for him?

The birds outside chirp with excitement. I stretch my knotted muscles. I should stop sleeping in the reclining chair. I walk to the window and notice snow in different stages of melting. It lingers in the shaded areas. Spring is nearly here, and for some reason, it makes me feel almost hopeful.

I heat a bowl of oatmeal, watch ten minutes of television, and drink two cups of coffee. My usual routine isn't satisfying me the way it should. I need some fresh air. I dress myself and find the P.O. Box key. I consciously block the thoughts of my last outing from my mind.

The truck starts after some hesitation. I drive down Father's road slowly, admiring the land. I'd like to go explore again, but I'm nervous I might run into another psychotic squirrel.

The parking lot at the post office is full, so I wait. Someone finally pulls out, and I squeeze the old truck into the small space. I slide out, careful not to hit the minivan next to me. There are children in the van. A few are strapped into child seats. An older child crouches in the middle and hands a toy to a toddler. Despite the closed windows, the tiny, happy sounds of their voices escape. I want to watch them. I imagine what it would feel like to be in a happy family, but one is staring at me. I don't want to look like a creep.

I walk into the post office. The wall of post office boxes looms tall. The number 209 is scribbled in permanent marker on Father's key. It takes me a moment, but I find the corresponding small door and squat down to open it. Mail is stuffed in it. I pull it out and clutch it in my arm. I stand and bump into a woman opening a box above mine.

"I'm so sorry," I say to the woman. Her eyes are captivating, and I can't look away from their green beauty. They stun me speechless.

"It's o—" Before the woman can complete her sentence, her voice is overtaken by a loud tornado-wind sound.

I know that sound. No, not again.

My body is frozen. I can't move my eyes. Intense pressure closes around me. Everything but the woman's eyes swirl into black nothingness. I feel the pulling of some unseen power. It all seems faster this time. As I am being pulled into her through her eyes. I try to call out, but my mouth is no longer my own, "God, make it stop," I say in my mind. He doesn't. Then I ask, "Why?"

Everything is black. I hear running feet and quick breaths. My heart pounds hard and I see that I am running. I look down long enough to know that these are not my legs or feet. Anxiety and fear fill me. The body that I'm in runs toward a busy neighborhood road that I don't recognize.

I try to stop the movement, it scares me, but I am not in control of this body. Parked cars line the street, and moving cars snake down the road, their drivers on their way to work, I suppose, by the slant of the sun. Adrenaline pumps through the body, but I have no idea why. Is the woman running from some unseen person?

A woman's voice screams, "No, stay there! Mama's coming!" The legs continue to run, tight with tension, fueled by fear. "Stay there!" the voice commands.

A toddler stands on the other side of the street looking at me, smiling. "Mama!" The toddler waves happily, oblivious to the urgency in the woman's voice. He starts to walk toward the road.

"Stay there!" the woman yells. The words ring through my head. The screaming hurts her throat. Her legs stop abruptly as a car rushes by followed by another spike of adrenaline in the woman's body. The body sprints across the street to the toddler. The woman scoops him up. He is in my arms, and I can feel the warmth between the woman's body and the toddler. Such tenderness fills me that I want to cry, but it is not within my power.

Then anger bubbles up. "Georgy, don't ever do that again! You CAN NOT cross the street by yourself." Wetness streams down the woman's cheeks, yet I feel a smile cross our lips. A powerful mix of emotions explode within her—worry, joy, sadness, and complete love—simultaneously. How can she handle all this at once?

"Poopy, Mama."

"I know, I see the puppy." The woman turns her head to look at a puppy behind a fence. "You can't come see it alone. Do you understand? You could get hurt."

The woman's arms squeeze the little boy tightly, and I feel her relief and intense love. They are emotions that I don't understand. The woman loves this child with more than just her heart. Is it her soul? I don't know. All I know is that it is beautiful.

The woman picks up the boy, and I notice pressure where his leg dangles across our stomach. Then I notice the tight feeling around the woman's midsection. I can't look down completely, but still I can see the bulge of pregnancy. The woman crosses the street and walks toward two children who look at her with concern.

"It's okay. But we've all got to watch Georgy. He's obsessed with that puppy."

"Can we stay outside, Mommy?" asks the little girl standing before her.

"Sure, but we'll go in the backyard."

We walk to a fenced-in, small backyard. It's strange moving like this. I feel like a marionette. The woman sits down, still holding the toddler. The morning air brushes across our face, crisp and warm, like the coming of summer.

"You," a finger touches the toddler's nose tenderly, "have got to stay with Mama when we drop Sarah off at the bus stop. No puppy without Mama."

The toddler looks at the mother, at my watching eyes, so tenderly that it hurts. "Otay, mama."

The child quickly changes moods and climbs off our lap to play with his brother and sister. They run around the yard in some game of chase only they understand. The woman runs her hand across her belly, caresses it. "Not long now, little girl, and you'll be playing with them too," she says. Her voice sounds exhausted.

I hear the woman's voice, although her lips are still. It must be her internal voice. *Thank you for all my children. Please keep them safe from harm. Thank you for keeping Georgy safe today. I don't deserve them, but thank you, God.*

An intense warmth courses through the woman's body. I think it's love.

The loud wind sound blasts in my ears and suddenly, as if thrown there, I inhabit my own body again. Now I look at the woman's eyes from the outside. "Sorry," I barely spit out.

"No worries, I'm fine," the woman says, rubbing her belly, which looks stretched to maximum capacity.

I push out the post office doors, gripping the mail tightly in my sweaty hands. The children in the van next to Father's truck are the woman's children. One of them sings a song out of tune. They look happy.

An unfamiliar mix of emotions runs through me as I climb into the truck and drive away. I can't make sense of it all. I am afraid of whatever strange thing is happening to me, but I also feel hopeful that there is that kind of love out there, it exists. I've always seen the world as full of evil. The happy bits have always seemed contrived by people who wanted to convince themselves that things don't suck.

A country song plays on the radio. I haven't heard this song since I was a teenager. I open my mouth and joyfully sing along. I haven't sung with the radio in years. Then I wonder, why not?

{4}

Friendship

The stack of mail rests in my lap. I look at my father, wondering if I really need to sort it or if I can simply throw it all away. I choose the responsible path, and my fingers begin their work.

"I guess you don't need these coupons for around town. Gas bill, electric bill, junk mail, more junk mail. What a waste of trees."

The intensity of the woman's love from the post office keeps poking at my mind. It makes me think of all the ways things could have been different.

"You know, Dad, it didn't have to be that way. I'm sure you missed her, but what about me? Did you even think about me? I mean—"

The doorbell rings, interrupting my thoughts and my sorting.

I walk to the front door, slightly annoyed by the intrusion. I open the door to find a young girl standing there, staring at me. Her blonde hair gleams in the sunlight. She stands with a hand on her hip, tapping her foot.

"Does the little girl who lives here want to play?" the girl asks.

I blink hard against the sun. "Who?"

"You know, the little girl." The girl lifts her eyebrows with the question.

"I'm sorry, but no little girl lives here. Who told you that?"

"My grandma. I'm staying with her for a while. She lives in the big yellow house just down the road. She said that a little girl lives here, and I should see if she wants to play."

"No little girls live here. You should go back to your grandma's house." The girl stands there, staring at me, so I slowly push the door shut, hoping she'll get the message and go. Before it shuts, a little hand reaches out and stops the door.

"What about you then? You want to play?"

"If you haven't noticed, I'm too big to play. Anyway, haven't you ever been told not to hang out with strangers, much less go knocking on their doors? Go back to your grandma." I shut the door.

The girl starts knocking persistently, then harder—much harder—than I thought a child could.

I roll my eyes and open the door again. "Look, I'm kinda busy—"

The girl reaches into her pocket and offers me some coins.

"Here. Hold out your hand."

I stand motionless. I am not going to be bribed by a few quarters and some pocket fuzz.

"Come on," the girl insists. "Hold out your hand."

I don't want to, but maybe she'll go away if I do. She drops the coins and lint into my hand.

"There. Now you can babysit me. My grandma needs some quiet. I can call her if you'd like. What do you say?" The girl smiles with more confidence than someone her age has a right to.

"Babysit?"

"Yeah, haven't you ever watched a kid before? I won't be much trouble. Promise. Come on, lady. Pleeeease?"

I want her to leave, but I also find her annoying ways entertaining. After all that's happened, I could use a distraction.

"Fine. Call your grandma. Tell her you're at the Clarks' house. Who is your grandma?"

"Josie Westly. She knows your dad."

"Well, tell her you're here. Ask her if she wants you to come home. I'm sure she will. Then do what she asks, no lying."

"Ok, I promise." The girl pushes the door open further and walks through the front hall and into the kitchen like she owns the place. She picks up the phone and dials expertly while she stares at me.

"Hi Grandma, it's me. I'm at the Clarks' house. Yes, his daughter is here, and she said she'd be happy to watch me so that you can rest." There is a pause. "I will. I won't. Okay. Bye."

The girl hangs up the phone and moves closer to me. "She said it's fine. Now, how about we go do something? It's dusty in here, and that man," she points to my father in the living room, "is scaring me just a little. Not too much."

She walks outside, and without much thought, I follow her.

"Do you have a name?" I ask as we walk out the door.

"Of course, that's silly. Everyone has a name." The little girl strolls toward the back property.

"Well, what is it?"

"Adrienne Marie Salstock. And yours?"

"I'm Amy. Amy Clark."

"Middle name?"

"Julia."

"Now that we know each other, we can play."

"I wouldn't say—"

She bolts down the path. Maybe I should let her run away and get back to sorting the mail. But, what if she gets lost? The way things are going, that probably *will* happen. I quicken my pace and follow her.

I can't see where she's gone to. "Adrienne, where are you?"

The girl jumps out from behind a wide oak tree. "Boo!" she yells. "Got you!" She sprints away, howling with laughter.

What's so funny about scaring someone to death?

I continue to follow her because I don't want her to get lost. How would I explain that to her grandmother?

Again Adrienne jumps out from hiding. It makes me jump.

"You got me! How about a break? I can barely breathe."

Adrienne shrugs her shoulders. "Okay." She skips toward the stream. I watch her settle her small body onto the large log the squirrel had taunted me from days before.

"So, what's your favorite sandwich?" Adrienne asks as I seat myself on the other side of the fallen log.

"Ham and cheese," I answer. The girl stares at me expectantly. What does she want from me?

"Now you ask me what's mine."

"What's your favorite sandwich?" I ask.

"P-B-J-B."

"You mean P-B-J?"

"Nope, P-B-J-B. Peanut butter jelly banana. It's delicious!"

We sit in silence. The sound of the stream calms me.

"Why is your dad hooked up to machines in your living room?" Adrienne asks.

"He's sick."

"Is he dying?"

"Yes, he is," I say, deciding that honesty is best.

"Too bad, sorry. My mommy just died. We were in a car accident."

"What? Oh my, I'm so...I'm so sorry, Adrienne. That is awful."

"It is. I miss her. She's in heaven now. Sometimes I see her smiling at me."

"You mean you actually *see* her."

"Uh-huh. Don't you see things like that?"

"No. But lately, I don't know. Things definitely aren't normal."

"How do you know?"

"I've been around for a while. I have a good idea of what normal is."

Adrienne's bright blue eyes stare at me too long. It makes me uncomfortable. The girl squeezes her lips together as if she has something sour in her mouth. Then she lifts one eyebrow and squints in a playful way.

"Okay, we know each other real good now. Time to play! You're it." Her blonde hair sways behind her as she runs away.

"Wait. I don't play tag. I don't…"

"You do now!" Adrienne yells over her shoulder. "You have to come find me."

I run into the woods. I don't want to play, but I have this nagging fear that she will get lost. The light is dim in the thick woods. The ground makes squishing noises against my feet. A cool breeze brushes my cheeks.

"Adrienne," I call.

I run from tree to tree, peering around their wide trunks, looking for the little girl. I climb over a fallen cedar and find her crouching behind it. I tag her and run. I zig-zag around trees and finally stop behind a large one. I slide down to crouch and catch my breath. It is very strange to play hide and seek with a stranger, but I am kind of having fun.

Adrienne tags me, and I laugh hard while I chase her again. My legs burn from the race; my cheeks tingle from smiling.

So this is what it's like to have a friend. I wish I had some more.

"Let's rest," Adrienne announces when I find her again. We sit down and catch our breath on a massive tree that must have fallen long ago.

"That was fun," I say. "Thanks."

"Let's—"

Adrienne doesn't finish her sentence. I look over at her. Something is different. The light around us grows piercingly bright. I close my eyes to protect them from the burn. I open them a tiny bit to see if Adrienne is okay. The girl is no longer solid; her body is translucent. I can see the log through her legs. Her silhouetted head looks up, her mouth moves as if she is talking to someone, but I don't hear any sound. My trembling hand reaches forward to grab Adrienne, to save her from whatever is happening. "Adrienne!" I yell. My arm goes right through her body. Adrienne becomes only light, then she disappears entirely.

I kneel at the spot Adrienne had been sitting in, but nothing is there, not even the light. I cradle my head in my hands and unleash a scream of horror and confusion. "Adrienne, what happened to you?"

I cry into my hands, using the log to support me. Something crawls across my arm. I look up, but I don't know what to do. There was a little girl here moments ago, and now she's gone. She disappeared right before my eyes. That doesn't happen to normal people. "God, I don't know what is happening. But if you exist, please help me. Don't let this go on. I can't handle it, whatever it is. Make it stop. Take me now. Let me die." I lay my head against the log and let my fears release through my tears.

"Why are you crying?" Adrienne's voice asks.

I look up to see the girl sitting further down the log, like she'd never left. Her eyebrows lift with concern.

"Where did you go?"

"I'm right here," Adrienne answers.

"You were gone. You...you disappeared."

"Oh, maybe that was when I was talking to Mommy."

"You were...talking to your mom?"

"She told me to come back. She said you needed some-one to play with. Don't be sad. I'm fine." Adrienne stands up on the log, balances on one leg, and smiles. "See?"

A deep sigh escapes from within me. My eyes ache, and my head throbs. I stand and rub my forehead with my fingers. What the hell just happened? What is happening to me?

"You're right, you look fine. You know, all the running has tired me out. I'm going to go home now. You'd better go back to your grandma's."

"Okay. Can we play later?"

"Sorry, I have stuff to do."

"How about tomorrow?"

"I'm not going to be here," I decide that instant. "I'm going home tomorrow. So…well…best of luck to you."

"I'll stop by anyway," Adrienne says as we walk to-ward the back of the house, "in case you change your mind."

"I won't."

"Just in case."

I stop and look at the girl's freckled face. "I won't be here, but do what you want. Just make sure to tell your grandma."

"Bye," the little girl calls as she skips down the drive-way.

***

I shove the door open and head straight to the guest room. I hoist my duffel bag onto the bed and pile all my clothes into it. How did this bag even get here? I have no idea, but it's time to fill it and go home. I've had enough. I find my coat, deodorant, brush—all of which I have no memory of bringing—and cram them all in. I'm tired of wondering what's going on. I'm tired of staring at my dying father. I'm done giving in to crazy. Whatever is going on, I'm done with it.

The hard part is saying goodbye. I tread quietly into the living room, wondering what words will suffice. I sit at the foot of his bed; I look away from him. Heaviness sits in my heart. I lean my head back, looking up at the ceiling. There are no answers there. I'm out of time. I want to leave before the nurse returns and I have to explain my abandonment. I force myself to look at him. I swallow down my guilt. It's unfortunate luck to have a daughter who would leave at such a time, but I think he helped make me this way. Nonetheless, I know it's wrong to leave.

"I know most of our times were rough. I'm sorry Dad. I'm sorry that you're sick and dying. I'm sorry that we never understood each other. I'm sorry for lots of things. Right now, I'm sorry because I have to go. I can't stay here anymore. I don't know what's going on, but it's not good. Something about this place is making me lose my mind. You probably won't even notice that I'm gone, but I still feel bad about leaving." Reluctantly, I pick up his hand. Its heaviness and warmth surprises me. I lift his hand to my lips and kiss it, then hold it against my check.

"Sorry, Dad. I'll miss you."

His finger twitches ever so slightly in my hand. I pull his hand away from my cheek and stare at it. Nothing. I look at his face closely. Nothing changes. It must have been my imagination.

I hold his hand and try to think of the right words to say goodbye. I feel his finger move again. This time I'm certain. His lips move slowly, as if he's thirsty. He squeezes his closed eyelids tight. His eyes open a tiny crack and he looks at me with vacant eyes. A look of recognition crosses his face, and the right side of his lips curl up in a small smile. He grumbles something incoherent and continues to smile. His eyes light up at me.

Thank goodness. But what do I do now? I still have to go. Leaving is the only hope I have of making the madness stop. If I stay, the downward spiral continues. If I leave, maybe, just maybe it will push things back to normal or some approximation of it. I'll feel like shit for the rest of my life if I desert him, but I can't take this anymore. I've got to do something to try to change my situation.

I decide that I'll sit with him while he's awake. He seems completely focused on me. His eyes stay on mine. "Ammmm," he says. I think he's trying to say my name.

His face sags. He looks exhausted. "It's okay, Dad. Go to sleep." He does.

I know I'm going to regret this, but I have no other choice. I find a piece of paper and a pencil in the kitchen and leave a note for the nurses telling them that something came up, and I have to go home.

I know I'm a bad person, a cold-hearted one. But what good am I to him if I'm just walking around talking gibberish? That won't help him. Either way, I've got to look out for myself. No one else does.

I grab my bag and pound toward Father's truck. He won't need it anymore anyway. I sit inside it with the key in the ignition, wondering. Could I stay? No, I can't. I'd rather be dead than endure any more of this disturbing descent. I turn the key, and the engine hesitates for a long moment. Then the engine coughs to life. My breath quickens. Cold air fills my lungs. I put all my energy into driving and pushing away the nagging feeling that it's wrong to leave my dying father.

***

The backcountry driving and empty expressways make me tired. I catch myself nodding off, and it revs up my adrenaline. I know the boost won't last long, so I roll down the window and let the cold air tear across my face. Despite my growing goosebumps I still feel exhausted, so I pull over at the next exit.

I drive into a desolate gas station. If the lit-up sign didn't say Open, I would have driven right past. When I walk in, my nose is assaulted by an antiseptic smell. It smells more of hospital than gas station. A male cashier stands behind the counter. He stares at me. I walk to the coffee station. The coffee looks and smells bitter and old, but it will do the job. I pour in extra cream and some sugar to make it palatable. The man behind the counter continues to stare. I say hello to reduce the awkward feeling. He doesn't respond. He's freaking me out, but I've come this far, and I need the coffee. I avoid his eyes and hand him money for coffee and gas. I walk out quickly.

I pump gas into the truck and drive back to the expressway. There are no cars out tonight. I drink the bitter coffee. My throat clenches against the acidity. I keep the window cracked to continue my wakefulness. I won't stop until I reach my apartment in Chicago.

Thoughts of the past week's strangeness bombard me. I let the thoughts flow, deciding it might help me fight sleep. Memories bubble up in my mind—the voices, Adrienne, the squirrel, being inside people, the awful rape—these things don't happen to sane people. Maybe it *is* just grief, but it seems like something more. All I can hope is that when I get home, the mind trip will stop.

I reach Highway 31 and finally see another car, then nothing. Darkness settles in, and all that holds it back are my headlights. The forest on the side of the expressway looks thick. Signs for Grand Rapids flash by, and I know in an hour I will start to see civilization. The headlights reflect on something. I slow down and see glowing eyes and the white tail of a deer. It disappears into the woods. I watch the deer retreat and look up to see another one standing in the middle of the highway. I grip the steering wheel and slam the brakes, turning the wheel to avoid the deer only to find another one in my path. I crank the steering wheel hard to the right. The truck veers toward the woods. I wrench the wheel in the other direction, but it doesn't respond.

Time slows. I see a tree racing toward the front bumper. I hear the crunch of metal and see the explosion of glass. How can breaking glass look so beautiful? Then my head veers toward the steering wheel. I reach my hands out but they are painfully slow. My head smashes against the steering wheel. I hear a sickening crunch.

***

I wake up in Father's house. I look around the guestroom and my things are spread out the same as they were before I packed them. I touch my face, lift my shirt, and peek under my pajama bottoms. Not a single bruise, but my muscles feel tight like I've been tensing them for days. I should be happy I'm alive, that wreck could have easily killed me, but what's the point of living in a nightmare like this? Sometimes bad things happen, and in the end, people see that it was for the best (at least I've read that in books), but there is no best here, only a freakish nightmare. This is not fair.

The truck has to be smashed. I run to the garage. Cold cement jolts my feet as I stand in front of Dad's old truck. The front is not damaged by anything more than rust and dirt. How can this be? It was not a dream—I packed my things, I drove the truck, I felt the sting of glass and the pain of smashing my head. It was not a dream! A powerful rage wells up inside me. I've never experienced such anger in all my life. I start pounding on the truck, screaming at whoever will listen. "Damn you, world, God, whoever is doing this. How can this be? I don't deserve this torture. MAKE IT STOP!" I keep pounding until my hands burn with pain. I slump onto the hood and rest, unsure of what to do next. What does one do when reality exits their life?

I retreat from the garage and mindlessly move toward the kitchen. I feel strangely disconnected from my body. It almost feels like…those times I was inside other people's bodies, like I am a spectator watching my arms move to make coffee and oatmeal. I turn the news on with the pliers and eat a banana with my oatmeal. It tastes like mushy nothing. Routine is doing me no good here.

I sit and watch my father. He is probably more in tune with reality in his state than I am in mine. "I don't know what the hell is going on here, Dad, but I'm leaving again, and this time I'm not coming back." I pick up his limp hand. "So, this time it's goodbye for good. I hope you're at peace. I'm sorry, I just need to get out of here. I don't know if you'd understand or not, but it's something I have to do." I look outside at the forest for a long time. "Dad, I want to say, for what it's worth, I'm sorry that things weren't different between us. It must have been hard for you, too. I guess I never really thought about that."

I pack my bag again, unsure if there is any point in it, but it seems the right thing to do. A strong sense of déjà vu sets in. Everything seems the same: the way my legs feel on the seat, the way my bag lies next to me in the truck, the hesitation of the engine. The ancient garage door lifts in the same lethargic way. I back out slowly, careful not to hit the bushes close to the driveway, and I notice Adrienne standing there, her hands on her hips again, as if she is ready to scold me. What does *she* want? She waves her arms dramatically for attention, so I stop and crank down the window.

"Where are you going? Can I come?" she asks.

"What are you doing up this early? Never mind. I'm going home, so no, you can't come. Sorry."

"What do you mean you're going home?"

"Um, usually that means that one is going to their *home*."

"You can't. It's not time to for you to leave yet."

"What on earth do you mean?"

"You need to stay," Adrienne insists.

"Didn't anyone tell you that it's not polite to talk to adults like that? I'm sorry, you'll have to find someone else to bother. Now, I need to go so I can get an early start. Don't you have school or somewhere you should be?"

I roll up my window. Adrienne goes on about why I can't leave. Her arms wave frantically, and her mouth moves. I can't hear her anymore though. Her eyebrows furrow in what looks like serious concern. That girl may be as crazy as I am. As I drive away, I see her arms and mouth still moving.

***

My legs and body are tired when I arrive at my apartment, but they are whole and intact. No suicidal deer, and no slumbering driver. I am here. Finally. Maybe this will be an end to it all. What "all" means, I don't want to think too much about. I have spent the day driving and trying my best to avoid thinking about any of it. These events need to be buried and forgotten. That is the only way I can survive.

I unlock my door and Fluffers runs to me, meowing piteously and rubbing against my leg. I reach down and lift my fat cat into my arms. "Oh, Fluffers, my sweet, sweet baby. Thank goodness they took good care of you. It doesn't look like you lost any weight. Still, let's get you some food." I drop my bag and stride into the kitchen to fill the cat's bowl with food. The food and water bowls are full.

"Looks like the pet sitters weren't here long ago." Fluffers rubs against my leg persistently.

A bag of cheap cat food sits next to Fluffers' bowls. Why would they feed him this cheap crap when I specifically told the super to tell them the good stuff? I find a few new cat toys in the kitchen. They went above and beyond in that respect.

In the bathroom, my hand towels are hung haphazardly. I am very particular about hand towels and would never leave them that way. Why are the pet sitters using my bathroom?

The two plants that sit on my wide windowsill aren't dead or dry. I've been gone for, as far as I can guess, almost two weeks. They would at least be stressed. I'm surprised they would water my plants. I know the super wouldn't have done that, it had to be the pet sitters. I'll have to give them a big tip.

My mind is overloaded. I want to work through all that has happened, but I don't know where to begin or how to process it all. I lie on my soft couch with Fluffers purring against my stomach, wondering what has happened, what is happening. Being at home is so comforting that I wonder if maybe it was only grief messing with my mind or maybe I had a feverish flu and couldn't think straight for a while. I don't know. I can only hope that there is some reasonable explanation for it all that doesn't end with me in a straightjacket. I close my eyes. I'm exhausted and spent in every sense of the word.

When I open my eyes, I am sitting in the chair beside my father.

***

It is dark in Father's living room, just like when I fell asleep in Chicago. I guess that's something—at least time is sort of constant. Obviously, I can't go home. But why? I pull on my shoes, which are sitting next to me though I can't remember putting them there, and find a flashlight.

The only person who seems to have any inkling of what is going on is Adrienne. She told me that I wasn't supposed to leave yet, so maybe she knows something about what's happening to me. I walk outside to the kind of pitch black that turns stars into diamonds. If I wasn't so pumped up on adrenaline, I might take a moment to appreciate them. I walk down the dirt road and feel strangely invigorated by the cool night air.

As I get closer to Adrienne's grandmother's house, I cover the flashlight with my hand to reduce the brightness. I want to see in front of me, but I don't want to announce to the world that I'm prowling in the night, since it's not uncommon for people who live in these parts to own guns. I need to figure out which window belongs to Adrienne without waking her grandmother. I stalk around the house, trying to figure out where the bedrooms must be. The living room windows are naked, without coverings, so I walk around to the back of the house. There is a window with doily curtains, and I guess that might be her grandmother's room. I move and find a windowsill that has a doll sitting on it. There's a good chance this is the one, so I knock softly. If it is the old woman, so what? Getting shot might not be bad if it puts an end to this nonsense. I knock again and wait. The curtains move, and I shine the light on myself so whoever is there can see that it's me. The curtains swish and the window squeaks open.

"What are you doing?" Adrienne asks, her eyelids heavy with sleep.

"Tell me what you meant," I ask.

"Meant by what?"

"You said it wasn't time for me to go. What did you mean?"

"I don't know what you're talking about."

"Cut the crap, little girl. You were standing in the driveway when I drove away this morning. You told me it wasn't time for me to leave, and you'd better tell me why."

"I don't—"

"Tell me!" I shout, louder than I mean to.

The girl turns her head toward something inside.

Adrienne whispers, "Grandma's coming. I've got to go." With that she shuts the window and closes the shade. I turn off my flashlight and walk slowly, feeling my way through the darkness.

{5}

Feeling

"This is fucked up." Whiskey pours golden brown into my glass. My father lies unmoving in the hospital bed. "I don't deserve this. I've been a good person. I haven't hurt anyone. I've minded my own business, and here I am in the *Twilight Zone* or some crazy shit." I pace the room, but it gets me nowhere. "I've got to get out of here. Whiskey sucks, and I need something else to drink."

I drive into town and find a bar. I've never been to this bar because I wasn't legal drinking age when I lived here, and I haven't spent much time in Roscommon since I moved away. The lights shine on the name: The Watering Hole. My plan is to drink as much as is necessary to put a fog in my mind that will keep all thoughts at a distance.

The bar is fairly dark and smells of stale beer. My legs tingle with nervousness. I've never even sat at a bar before, much less drank at a bar alone. Or even drank much at all, until now. I find a stool near the far end, away from the other patrons, and perch on it. The mirror behind the bar reflects the small dim lights that adorn it, which wear the dust of many months. A woman in a tight T-shirt, jeans, and half-apron approaches me from behind the bar.

"Hey, what can I get ya?"

"How about something that tastes good but packs a punch. Got anything like that?"

"I'll mix something up for you. How does that sound?"

"Good," I say. My hands fidget with my purse while I wait.

The woman comes back with a purple-colored drink on ice.

"Give it a try," she says.

I take a sip. It is sour but sweet. My mouth tingles with the aftertaste of alcohol. "That'll work. How about mixing me another one? This one won't last long," I say and then I start to drink it.

The mirror allows me to watch the other patrons on the sly. I hope no one will bother me, but I need distraction, so I watch the others and imagine their conversations. The first and second drink slide down fast, but the third drink is slower, as I feel the bubbling of alcohol coursing warm through my veins.

A man from the other side of the bar walks toward me. I make a silent wish for him to walk straight past...and he does, moving down the hall, which leads to the restrooms. Relief floods through me. The last thing I want is conversation. The TV flashes numbers for a lottery game. My drink stands empty again. The man from the restroom comes out and sits next to me.

"Hey, I don't remember seeing you here before."

"That's because I don't come here. Sorry, but I'm not in the mood for company."

"No need to be rude, now. I'm just stopping to say hello."

"Hello. Now go away."

He stares at me, but I will not look back. Alcohol smell seeps from his skin. He reeks of it. A woman sits on my right in the last barstool.

"You might be alone for a reason, acting like that," the man continues.

"Just go away. I don't feel like talking," I tell him.

"I just—"

The woman next to me speaks up. "I believe my friend here said she wants to be left alone."

I look at over at the woman. She has long, dark brown hair. Her skin shines the color of honey. A black shirt fits tightly over her breasts. One eyebrow lifts with attitude. "Just because a girl wants to sit and have a drink doesn't mean she wants to be bothered, Hank. Now shoo."

"Okay, fine. I guess I'm outnumbered. If you change your mind," he looks at me suggestively, "I'll be right down there," he points to the other end of the bar and saunters away.

"Thanks for that," I say to the woman.

"You don't have to thank me. I know how it is. Hank knows I have a boyfriend, but he still pesters me when I come in. He needs to learn some manners."

I smile, unsure of what else to say.

"So, are you from around here?" the woman asks.

"No. I'm visiting my dad."

"Well, good to have you here. It can get lonely at the bar with all these guys," she says, nodding her head toward the men at the other end. "They think they own this place."

The bartender comes to take the woman's order.

"My name's Jenna, what's yours?"

"Amy."

"Well, nice to meet you. Would you like to do a shot with me? Looks like you could use another drink."

I look down and remember my empty glass. "Sure."

We order and gulp. It burns.

An uncomfortable silence grows. I'm not sure if I should be making small talk. That's not something I'm good at.

"I'm just waiting for my boyfriend, David. He works second shift and sometimes we meet here before we…hang out."

"Oh, that's nice." Jenna seems kind, but I want her to leave. She did save me from being harassed, but I need to be alone.

"You see, it *is* very nice…if you catch my drift." I look at the woman to see if I can catch her drift. Is she talking about sex? Her eyes are a beautiful brown. She has long eyelashes.

The whooshing sound that I dread so much grows in the distance until it is billowing against my ears. Obviously the woman doesn't hear it. My eyes lock in vision tunnels toward her eyes, unable to move. I feel the familiar pull and pressure and know that I'm being transported.

Everything is dark and silent. Warmth radiates between her legs. I have never felt such heat. A woman, presumably Jenna, moans softly. A deeper moaning follows—a man's voice.

I open my eyes and see a man supporting his upper body with his muscled arms. He gently rocks against us, thrusts himself inside. His sculpted body glistens with sweat. He is handsome in a rugged way with disheveled, short brown hair and the early growth of a beard. The man stares into the woman's eyes. I feel embarrassed, thinking he will realize that I am not his girlfriend.

"Do you like that?" he asks.

"Yeah," I hear Jenna's voice respond.

Is this what it's supposed to feel like? I remember my two failed attempts at love making: the first time drunk at a college party with a boy I'd dated for a few months. It lacked anything but embarrassment and pain. It made me wonder why people make such a fuss over sex. The time with Tommy seemed like it might have been better, but I don't remember much of it, and after I'd felt certain that it had been a mistake.

This is different. Jenna's body burns with sensuality. Every thrust brings a deeper sensation of joy within her, not only in her body, but in her heart. Her heart beats so wildly that I can hear the pulse of it in her ears. Her body is all warmth and emotion. Could this sensation, this feeling, be love?

Jenna's moaning becomes more urgent. I feel her move the angle of her hips. The man moves more swiftly in response. Something is happening to Jenna's body. The warmth between her legs turns to jolting joy that pulses throughout her body, briefly, but intensely—waves of it course through her. I have never experienced anything like it before. *Jenna must be having an orgasm.* I feel a bit cheated. That is not what my romps with Joey Davison and Tommy had been like, not even close.

Jenna's body moves closer to the man. She wraps her arms around his naked body. His pulse beats so hard through his skin that I can feel it. The lovers breathe deeply catching their breath after the marathon of sex. The man opens his eyes and looks at me. His eyes are mesmerizing. I could look at them forever. His lips curl in a tired, handsome smile.

"I love you, babe."

"I love you, too," Jenna's voice says.

I close my eyes. Why haven't I ever found anything like this? All this time, I thought people were exaggerating—I thought it was all a bullshit notion of love portrayed in Hollywood movies. Why else would most marriages end in divorce? Now, I see that I might have been wrong. Being alone might have saved me from pain, but it has also kept me from love.

The whooshing sound returns, and I am back in my body. I open my eyes and see Jenna looking at me with confusion.

"Hey, girl. Did you daze out for a minute or what? You okay?" She waves at the bartender. "How about a water down here?"

Jenna looks at me. "Why's your face so red? You look like you've been caught with your hand in the cookie jar."

"Um, I forgot. I need to be somewhere."

"Hey, you look tipsy. I could give you a ride before David gets here. Do you live far?"

"No." I grab my purse, throw a tip on the bar, and stand up. "Really, I'm fine. Nice talking to you."

I look straight forward and avoid the eyes of anyone else as I stagger out the door. My heart thumps wildly; I take a few deep breaths to slow it down. The brisk air and my racing heart make me believe I'm almost sober until I trip over an obvious pothole. Either way, I don't care. I need to leave.

I climb in Father's truck and cautiously pull away. I focus all my attention on driving the truck slowly. I know even if I crash, I probably won't die going 25 miles per hour, but you never know, and at the moment I'm not in the mood for death. The lines on the road are tricksters, moving around, messing with my mind. I pull over on a backroad. I can't drive. I rest my head on the steering wheel.

Sadness fills my heart. It is a sinking feeling with no bottom. Tears won't even do it justice. There is so much I'm sorry for: my dying Dad, not knowing my mother, this sudden disconnect between reality and sanity. Yet, what makes me feel utterly hopeless is that I have purposely chosen a life designed to keep people out. I thought I'd found the secret that everyone else refuses to acknowledge—that ultimately we are, and always will be, alone. Why pretend to care for people when they will die, deceive you, or not love you in return? I didn't want to pretend. I wanted structure. I wanted to eliminate the surprises and disappointment that comes from love. I was safe because loss, sadness, and rejection couldn't touch me. What did not occur to me, up until a few moments ago, is what I had given up. There *is* risk with love, but without the risk, you won't find it. And maybe, just maybe, it's worth having.

{6}

Awake

I wake with a cottony, sour alcohol taste in my mouth. I stretch and listen from the guest bedroom to the sounds of the house. It takes me a moment to realize that I never drove home last night but at this point, I hardly care, my emotions are growing numb.

Someone moves about in the kitchen, putting dishes away. Rhonda's voice sounds different. Why is she talking at all? Maybe another nurse is here, or maybe… I flop out of bed and jog to the kitchen despite my stabbing headache.

Rhonda turns toward me. The edges of her eyes lift with what looks like joy. "You'll never guess who's up," she says through her face mask.

My Father's hospital bed in the living room has been adjusted into a sitting position. All I can see is the back of it. "Dad?" I look at Rhonda. She is beaming.

Slowly, I walk to the living room, peek around the side of the bed, and see my dad, awake. His puffy eyes look back at me, and his lips lift into a smile.

He stares warmly at me.

"Dad! You're awake. It's a miracle. How are you doing? Do you need anything? Do you—"

"His voice is quite hoarse," Rhonda interrupts. "It might be awhile before he can say anything." She stands beside me, but I hadn't heard her move.

"Ugalifno…" Father says. His voice makes me wince. It sounds painful, like his voice box sits in sand.

I grab his hand. At first, it feels unnatural. We were never the touchy-feely type of family. I fight through the strangeness of it because Father's eyes somehow tell me that he needs comfort. He looks a little scared.

"Don't talk now, Dad. Save it for later." I hold his hand while he stares at me. "You're looking good dad," I lie. His eyes grow heavy and I watch him slowly fall asleep.

I let go of his hand. Suddenly I need some answers. I pad out of the room, motioning for Rhonda to follow. When we're out of earshot, I ask her, "What does it mean? Is he getting better?"

Rhonda breathes deeply, her eyes gracing the floor. "I'm afraid not. It doesn't change his diagnosis, but it's a miracle nonetheless."

"Oh."

"My advice? Enjoy the time you have with him. It may not be much, but it's extra time. Say anything that is left unsaid, comfort him, and say goodbye."

I don't know how to respond. Even if I did, the lump in my throat will not let me talk.

***

I have been watching Father all day, looking for some kind of meaning in his awakening. He drifts, like a ghost, between coherence and sleep. When he is alert, he makes urgent sounds that weave themselves into nothing, to both our disappointment. I try to fake comprehension with nods and assurances, but I'm not sure that it works. I wonder what is so important to him.

Right now, he snores softly. Rays of sunlight warm my legs. I feel a strange sense of peace despite all that has happened.

The doorbell rings, interrupting my calm moment. I walk to the door, ready to tell Adrienne to leave. I look through the peephole. I don't know the older woman on the other side.

I open the door, and the woman says in a voice much younger sounding than expected, "Hello." It must be a visitor from church I realize. I'm surprised that I haven't met any yet.

"Hello," I plaster a polite smile on my face although I'm not in the mood for laborious socializing. I hope the woman won't stay long.

"Hi. I don't think we've met. I'm Gertrude Sorrington. I'm Adrienne's grandmother."

I peek around the woman to see if Adrienne is with her.

"I live down the road. I'm friends with your father. I haven't seen him a while. I brought this." She lifts up the dish in her hand. "I'd like to see him if it's okay."

"Oh, I...well, you see..." I try to think of some reason not to let the woman in when Rhonda walks up behind me.

"Gerty, how *are* you doing? We haven't seen you in a while."

"Well, I had a little cold, and I figured that was the last thing Harold needed."

"You're right about that. Very thoughtful. Come on in. He'd love to see you." Rhonda gently opens the door for Gertrude to enter and takes the casserole from her hand. She guides Gertrude into the living room. "You'll never believe it, but Harold awoke yesterday. He hasn't been able to talk, but he seems at peace. He'll just be so happy to see you."

Resentment, thick as bile, bubbles up within me as I watch Gertrude make herself at home beside my father. She takes his hand into her shaking, wrinkled one, and holds it firmly against her cheek.

"Old friend, it's good to see you again."

Harold looks at her and smiles. He doesn't try to talk. She places his hand back by his side but keeps her hand on top of his.

"Your father and I have been friends for many years," she says, looking at me. "My husband and I moved up here ten years ago from Royal Oak, which is not too far from Detroit. We thought we would have a peaceful re- tirement here, away from the hubbub and so close to na- ture and such splendid beauty. We enjoyed it. For three years, we tried our hand at playing frontier people, in a way. We met your father through church and eventually became friends. He shared many dinners with us."

"That's nice," I say, but I don't mean it. My father never spoke of how close he was with Gertrude, but then again, what do I know about my father's life? Nothing, really. It's a reminder of how things are between us.

"Yes it was. My husband thought of your father as a son. We had daughters, you see, no boys. Anyway, when Claude died the fifth winter after we moved here, I thought I would die right along with him. I didn't see how I could live without him. We'd been together fifty-one years. When you lose someone you've been with that long, it's worse than losing limbs, I'd say. Anyway, your father helped me through it. Anyone else might not have been able to, but he could because he'd been through it himself."

I don't know what to say. My father helping others is not the man that I knew or know. He rarely spoke my mother's name in all my life, but he'd used his pain to help this woman? I can't decide if I'm touched or violently nauseated. Maybe both.

"I'm sorry for your loss," I say.

"And I for yours. It couldn't have been an easy thing to lose your mother at such a young age."

"No."

"Gulomph," Father says, tears well up in his eyes and sweep down his checks.

"I know, Harold, I know," Gertrude reassures him, patting his hand, as though she has heard words instead of incomprehensive grunts.

"He told me how hard it was for you. He told me so many things about you. He's a proud father you know. Anyway, for a long time, he kept me company with very few words, which was fine by me. I didn't want someone telling me how time would heal wounds or such rubbish. I try to do the same by him now. After years went by and I could talk again about my Claude, we shared our stories. He told me about his life with your mother, and I told him our story. It healed us both some, I'd say. Lovely stories too."

I can no longer meet Gertrude's eyes. How can a stranger know more about my mother and father than I do? It's too much. It disgusts me. I can't listen to it anymore. I stand and rub my eyes. I need to leave before my anger spills out. "It was nice to meet you. I have to…well, I have some things I need to do. You stay as long as you'd like."

Gertrude continues talking, she's insistent, like her granddaughter. "He was sorry. He thought he'd failed as a father and didn't know how to make it up. I told him to just say the words, but men aren't so good with that sometimes. I hope he can tell you himself before the end. He needs peace, you know."

"Okay, thanks…" I say as I leave the room quickly on my fictional, urgent task.

I sit on the edge of the bed, stupefied. I don't want to be angry with him anymore, but I can't help it. We were making progress before Gertrude showed up.

Now, I don't know how to feel except cheated out of a mother and a father. To hear that he felt one way and acted another confuses me. If he loves me, why didn't he ever show it? Why was he consistently cold and neglectful? That's not how you treat people that you care for. Why did he tell this woman about his feelings and not me? If he loved my mother, how come we weren't allowed to talk

about her? How could he keep the only things I wanted —
his attention and knowing about my mother –to himself?

***

My body feels drained, empty. This is too much emotion for me. I feel like I'm sinking into the guestroom bed.
I hear a soft knock. Should I ignore it? I drag my body to
the door and open it to see Gertrude.

"I wanted to say goodbye and to tell you that if you
need anything, anything at all, you should let me know.
Even if you run out of salt or need an egg or whatnot, I'll
send my granddaughter over if I'm not able."

"Adrienne."

"Oh yes, she did say that she met you. I nearly forgot.
Very nice. Well, let me know if you need anything, and I
see that you get it."

Those words, again: I see. "What did you—?" I look into Gertrude's knowing eyes—bright blue, wise, surrounded by sagging skin. The loud train-like whooshing sound
fills the room, pulling me out of my skin and body and
into Gertrude.

Before I can see, I hear the sound of persistent squeaking, like an unoiled door opening and closing. Something
warms the tops of our legs, maybe sunlight. The smell of
lilacs permeates the air. Gertrude's eyes open, and I can
see. I feel aches in her body –her back, her hands, her an-
kles—and I realize that Gertrude is already old and that
the world has been unkind to her body. We are sitting on
a large, wooden rocking chair on a porch. It's the same
porch that I saw in the dark only days before when I'd

gone looking for Adrienne. The lilac bushes dance in the sunlight, waving in the gentle breeze, which scatters their scent.

"Ah, spring," Gertrude comments.

"Beautiful thing, it is," a male voice responds. I didn't realize that we aren't alone. Gertrude looks to the right at an older man. It must be Claude.

"It never disappoints," Gertrude says.

"Indeed," the man agrees.

Gertrude is quiet, but her mind wraps itself around memories of past springs. It is a special season for her. Memories flash through her mind, intertwining with strong emotions, mostly love. I see the first spring she shared with Claude. Her love for him grew into intense yearning, which she took great effort to keep hidden. She wanted to kiss him for hours but only allowed him a short peck when no one was looking. The second spring she shared with him was when he proposed. Happy tears grace her eyes as she thinks about it.

Later springs make her think of her daughters. When they were young, spring arrived like a godsend after too much time trapped indoors. When they noticed the first spring blooms, it made the girls giddy, as though they had invented spring themselves.

Gertrude focuses on the lilac bushes that Claude had planted for her. He knew how she loved them, and he'd put his old body through great pains to get them into the ground. Her aching body grew warm at the thought of Claude's passion in the spring, which always seemed more robust than at any other time of year.

Claude smiles at us. "You're as beautiful as the first spring I met you."

"Oh, you're such a liar, old man," Gertrude chides him.

"Tis a fact."

"Well, I love you for saying it."

"I love you too."

Contentment courses through Gertrude's body. Somehow I understand that it wasn't a perfect life for her, but it had the constant undercurrent of love, and that gave Gertrude the strength to endure the pains and disappointments of life.

I feel the familiar pull and am soon returned to my body. Gertrude's eyes fill with tears. "Yes, I loved him, you see," she says and then slowly ambles off toward the front door.

***

The living room glows soft orange in the setting sun. I walk in and find that my father is awake. Somehow I sense that his time is near. The time has come to ask the question that bothers me most. I should probably keep my mouth closed, but I have to know. I sit on the edge of his bed.

"I need to ask you something Dad," I ask. "Why didn't you talk about her?"

"Her?" he asks, his voice still sounds hoarse and painful.

"Mom. You didn't talk about her. Why?"

"I don't...I didn't...know how." His eyes look wet. Are those tears?

I want so badly to tell him what he needs and wants to hear—tell him that it will be okay—but I can't. It wasn't okay. It isn't okay. I've wasted my life making up for his mistakes.

"You told Gertrude about her. You told her the story of how you and mom met. Don't you think that would be important to me? She was *my* mother."

"I'm sorry."

"I would have liked to have known more about her. It was like she never even existed."

"It was a...mistake." He coughs, clears his throat, "I see...I see that now."

I want to scream. I'm so tired of those words. What the hell do they mean?

"I tried my best. I failed you." He swallows thickly. "I loved her," he says.

Tears roll down his cheeks. I realize, in that moment, that it couldn't have been easy for him either. He didn't get to grow old with my mother. He didn't have the buffer of her love to get through the hard times. I realize that he was just as lost as I was without her. I always focused on my loss and didn't much consider his, but to be fair, he never talked about it.

"You didn't fail. You made a mistake."

He sobs. I wrap my arms around him. It's unfamiliar but warm. I am sorry for him. Sorry that his life didn't turn out the way he wanted. Mine didn't either, I can't change the past. It still hurts, but my father is dying. He needs something from me.

"I forgive you, Dad. Don't be sad. I forgive you. It's okay."

They are not empty words. I mean them. Saying those simple words lifts something inside me, some sort of darkness that has long weighed me down. They are powerful words.

The Light

I wake in the morning to heavy, slow moving limbs. Stacking my body upright drains my energy. Whatever is happening is starting to physically exhaust me.

My feet move like bricks as I clunk down the hall. I trip over them. The slant of the sun tells me that I've slept late into the morning. The light grows brighter as I enter the kitchen. My hand rises to shield my eyes.

I turn away from the light and toward the kitchen cupboards to begin my comfortable morning routine. Oatmeal dust drifts as I empty the package contents into a bowl. I pour some water over the oats, and start the microwave. My eyes are drawn to the golden light. It looks peculiar. It radiates from Father's bed instead of the window. The microwave beeps as I walk over to investigate.

I have to protect my eyes from the brightness. Father is lying in bed, smiling, transformed. He looks like a shell of himself, and that translucent shell contains the light. My eyes adjust until the brightness no longer hurts.

"Dad, what's going—"

Nurse Rhonda walks in through a door in the living room—a door that moments ago did not exist. More light radiates from Rhonda's skin.

I step back and stumble over my own feet. I don't understand what is happening. I look from my father to the nurse, hoping for answers. Words that want to form sentences tumble from my lips. "What...I...Dad?"

My father sits up easily, as if he had never been sick, and looks at me. Brightness glows from him.

"It's time, Amy. Time to go."

I sigh. "I knew this was coming. I knew something was wrong with me. I'm ready. I—"

"Not you." He shakes his head. "Me."

"I don't understand. What's going on? Why do you look like that?"

"I'm between going and gone, but it doesn't matter. What matters is that I get to say goodbye."

"How is this even possible? It doesn't make any sense."

"I know it's hard to understand. There's not enough time to explain. My time is almost done here. I'm not even sure that I *could* fully explain it."

"I don't know what to say except I'm sorry. I'll miss you."

"Don't be sorry for me. Where I'm going, things are much better than here. I've seen only a glimpse, but that was enough."

I stare at him and wonder why this is all happening to me. Is this even real? It doesn't seem possible. Everything has an ethereal quality, like a dream, but the objects around me are solid.

"I need to know that you truly forgive me. I'm sorry. I was not a good father. You deserved much better," he says.

"Of course. I do. I forgive you."

"Thank you, Amy. You also have to forgive the world for taking your mother too soon. It's time to move on. Truly live. I know I bear much of the blame, but please do this for me. For us. We want you to be happy."

"We?"

Dad looks to Nurse Rhonda. In her shiny brilliance, I didn't notice her missing facemask. My heartbeat quickens. How could I have been so blind? How could I not have noticed? Now I remember. Her first name was Rhonda, but everyone called her by her middle name, Lucy. I should have seen that it was her.

"Mom?"

"Amy, it has been my dream to spend time with you. I've watched you for a long time, so lost and lonely. You don't have to be alone. Ever. There are many others with us if we are open to them. I'm so happy to have seen you, my daughter. I love you."

Tears race down my face. All I've ever wanted is here, in this room, getting ready to leave.

"How could I not have seen that it was you? Why didn't you tell me? I could have been getting to know you. We could have—"

"You may not understand, but it wasn't the right time. You weren't ready."

I should be thankful for this opportunity, whether it's a dream or not, but I feel angry.

"Why now? I've needed you for so many years. Why didn't you come before?" My voice sounds like a whiny child, but I can't help it.

"I've always been with you, you just didn't notice."

"What? I don't understand. I've spent my whole life missing you, wanting a father who cared, who showed that he cared." My father's face sags with sadness. I'm the worst sort of person.

"You may not realize it yet, but right now you are open to more possibilities than you were before. It will all become clear to you. But for now, the time has come." She points to the new door. It opens more, revealing its piercing light.

"I'm sorry Mom; I'm sorry Dad." I've never felt such an urgency of time. I would give anything for more of it. They would soon be gone, and I'd squandered my short time. "Forgive me. I was too harsh, I'm sorry."

Father stands and walks to the door. "There's no need to be sorry, Amy. You need to let go. You need to forgive. Remember that we love you. We always will."

"I love you, Amy," Mother says. "Find peace, it is yours, you see."

"I love you both, too. Goodbye," I cry to their disappearing silhouettes as they walk through the door. The door vanishes, along with the light, and I am left alone with the late morning sun and my father's body.

***

The casket sits before me, shiny and cold. The heavy fragrance of flowers pierces the air and nauseates me. I shake the hands of strangers and wonder how I got here. The last few days have whizzed by in a blur. I'd nodded my head when asked about arrangements, and time ran by until today, the day of Dad's funeral. *His funeral.* The words echo in my mind, surreal and sad. Why hadn't I forgiven him sooner?

It all feels like a dream.

My thoughts and body are too heavy. I sit down. The upholstered chair sags uncomfortably.

I notice a small form moving toward me, wearing a black dress. Adrienne walks right up to me. Her brilliant blue eyes glisten with sadness.

"I'm sorry about your dad," she says as she sits next to me.

"Thanks."

"I have to go, but let's go outside first."

"Okay."

I mindlessly follow Adrienne, wondering what she wants but too exhausted to ask. We sit on a bench. The air is cool, but the sky is clear, and the sun shines warmly.

"You saw your mom, didn't you?" Adrienne asks.

"How did you know?"

"You see; I see."

"What did you just say?" My body tenses. I never want to hear those words again.

"I mean you saw your mom, and I saw my mom."

I stare at Adrienne for a long moment, looking for any hint of understanding. Did she know about my visions?

How could she? Why would she choose those exact words? What did it mean?

"You know," Adrienne says, "it's time to go."

"Okay, see you later." It will be a relief when she leaves. She unnerves me.

"No, it's time for *you* to go."

"Go where?"

Adrienne stands and steps in front of me, blocking the sun. I watch for any hint of what is going on. Maybe she's crazy too.

"I think you know," Adrienne says.

"Actually, I have no idea what you're talking about! Look, it's been a long day. I don't want to play any games right now." I lean forward, resting my head in one hand and rubbing my neck with the other.

"Amy, I'm not playing. This is very serious. You can get stuck here, you know."

I hear a beep. The same beep that I've heard off and on for days. It never stops. It must be a symptom of the psychotic spell I'm under.

"You're not crazy, Amy."

"How did you know—"

"There's no time to explain. You're not dreaming, and you're not awake. You are in-between. That's how we met. I'm in-between too. Everyone here is in-between life and death…or just plain dead. You can't stay in this place too long or you'll get stuck. Then it's really hard to get out. Sometimes impossible."

I sit up. My back is stiff, but my mind is alert. "It's finally happened. I've lost the last of my sanity." I look up to the clouds and ask, "God, how could you do this to me?"

"It's a gift. You've been given a gift. You may not remember any of this later, but you'll remember the emotions. You can change."

"How do you know all this? Are you an angel?"

"No, I'm not an angel. Not yet anyway. My mom's explained most of it. Some of it, I just know."

"I don't understand any of this. Is my dad really dead?"

"That part is true. But you missed his funeral."

"I missed it? But I'm right here," I say.

That's what I'm trying to tell you, you're not here. Your mind is, but you're not," Adrienne says matter-of-factly. "Do you hear that beeping? Do you know what that is?"

"I do hear it. I've heard it every day since I got here."

"That is the sound of where you *really* are, and you need to go back there now. I have to go back too."

"How come you know, and I don't?"

"There's no more time. Take my hand."

I don't want to. I'm too full of questions. I'm tired of not knowing, but I can't deny the urgency in Adrienne's eyes, and for some reason, I trust her. Adrienne is the first person in my adult life that I've trusted. Adrienne reaches for me with her small hand, and I wrap my fingers around it tightly. "Close your eyes," she says. I do.

Everything changes in that moment. Comfortable silence surrounds us. The birds outside go quiet, the murmur of nearby people hushes. All is silent. Somehow, there is beauty in the absence of sound. I didn't know such a thing existed.

Beep. Beep. Beep.

The sound returns, but this time it is persistent. I hear murmurs of a different type. The smell grows antiseptic. It smells of hospital.

"Where are we?" I open my eyes, but all remains black. I feel a hand in mine. Adrienne is still there. I squeeze her hand to let her know that I'm there.

"Oh my God!" I hear a man's voice exclaim. "She just squeezed my hand! Come quick! Amy squeezed my hand! Amy, do it again. Move your hand!"

Tommy? It sounds like his voice, but I'm not sure. I try to squeeze again, but instead I am overwhelmed with the desire to sleep.

{8}

Recover

I wake up to more beeping. I try to move, to get up, but some invisible force weighs me down. Finally, I can see, but I have to strain my eyes to focus and the dim light doesn't help. There is a monitor next to my bed flashing with fuzzy numbers. I struggle to move my arms. I can't. They are restrained by some kind of netting. There are tubes running from different parts of my body. My body, strangely, doesn't quite feel like my own. It doesn't obey my commands when I give them. My arms and legs jerk of their own volition.

The windowsill is covered in vases full of flowers. But it doesn't make any sense. Who would have brought me flowers? Worse yet, why am I in the hospital? Maybe my psychotic break surfaced in public, and they sent me here. I don't know. Maybe it's for the best. Maybe they can help me. I'm tired of all this hallucinating.

A whooshing sound erupts, startling me. I feel pressure around my legs and I look down to see black, stocking-like things wrapped around them. They are squeezing me. I'm scared that they'll hurt me, and my heart rate increases; I see proof of it on the monitor. A small plastic remote sits on the table next to me with a red nurse call button. It mocks me because my arms are not free. The netting around them reminds me of fishing net. I am caught. I begin to panic. Why am I here? This squeezing thing might kill me. I try to yell out but my voice doesn't work. It's broken. I have never felt such fear in all my life—not when my mother died, not when I hallucinated the rape, not ever. I am helpless and terrified. Unrelenting horror flows through me. How fast can a heart pump before it explodes? My mind races along with my heart, then I feel the deep pull of sleep. How can I be sleepy when I'm…

***

I open my eyes. Bright daylight seeps through the windows. It makes my eyes water, but I welcome its normalcy. Everything is blurry. There is a man sitting beside me, but I can't see his face, only the outline of his form.

The man yells, "She's awake again!" He jumps up and yells it again and again and runs out of the room. I hear other voices responding to his words. He comes back and hovers over the bed. Tommy?

"Amy, you're awake! Keep your eyes open. It's so good to—"

Good to what? I want to hear the rest, but sleepy darkness calls, and I'm powerless to resist.

***

"How are we doing today?" I hear the pleasant voice of a woman.

I try to talk, but it comes out, "Urgll." It doesn't sound like my voice.

Quick footsteps move toward my bed. The face of a red haired woman hovers over me. I see her!

"Well, hello there, Amy."

"Ughaa," I say. Why isn't my voice working? I take a deep breath and try again. "Ghuma."

"It's okay." She reaches out and pats my arm. "It takes time. Don't be too hard on yourself. No one comes out of a coma quoting Shakespeare. Don't believe what 'cha see in the movies, girl." The nurse lifts my left eyelid up high, shines a painfully bright light into it, and then does the same with the right. My eyes begin to water again.

Did she say *coma*?

"Speaking of Shakespeare, I'd better go get your Romeo." She gives me an exaggerated wink and leaves the room.

A moment later, the nurse returns. "He'll be along in a minute." Two more nurses and a doctor follow her into the room. They move around me, hover over me, and generally stare at me. They discuss me with words that I don't recognize. It makes little sense. I feel like a specimen under study. They all seem happier than they have a right to be considering I just found out that I've been in a coma.

When they finish examining me and file out of the room, I notice Tommy sitting in the chair next to my bed.

"Whfta?" is all I can say. Damn it, I have questions, but they refuse to come out!

"It's okay, Amy. They say your speech will come back, so don't worry. Do you remember anything?"

I shake my head. I'm not sure what he means, but even if I could talk, I wouldn't be telling the world about my psychotic break.

"Do you want me to tell you what happened?"

I'm scared to hear the answer, but I do want to know. I nod yes.

"Now?"

What other time were we talking about? I nod again.

"Are you sure? I don't want to upset you, but I know that *I'd* like to know."

I'm getting impatient. "Ysh," I say.

Tommy looks at me and nods in return. He puts his hands together in his lap, sits a little taller, and takes a deep breath. "First of all, you're going to be fine." He looks at me for a moment, his eyebrows lift with reassurance. "But a few weeks ago you had an accident. You were hit by a car. You're quite lucky, actually. Not because you were hit by a car, but because it could have been much, much worse. You fractured a rib, bruised yourself up, and hit your head pretty good. That's what caused the coma. The good news is that you're going to be okay."

"Ahh, is Sleeping Beauty awake?" I turn my head and see the nurse with the red hair.

"She looks good today," Tommy tells her.

Today? Why is he here now, much less yesterday or any other day?

"She's lucky to have such a prince. Your boyfriend's been by your side every day, Amy. You're a lucky girl."

"Friend," Tommy says, looking down.

"Huh?" the nurse asks, taking notes from the monitor and changing a bag near the underside of the bed.

"We're friends," Tommy says.

The nurse stands up with a plastic, fluid-filled bag in her hand. "Oh, I see," she says. "Well, maybe you'll be more than that before this is all over." She winks at me again and leaves the room.

I tilt my head in a questioning way, hoping that Tommy will give me some clue as to why he is here. He's saying something else, but the sleepy darkness pulls at me again. I can't fight it.

***

I think it's early morning the next time I open my eyes, but it's hard to grasp time right now. The sun is still low in the sky. Every time I open my eyes, I don't know if it will be day or night. Sleep has become my constant companion. I have other companions too—nurses, the occasional doctor, therapists, and Tommy.

I hear the clicking of high heels. A petite blonde woman walks into my room. She stands next to me, looking at me, waiting for something, although I'm not quite sure what.

"So, you must be Amy."

I nod.

"Well, my name's Jenny Plearington. You can call me Jenny."

I stare at her because there's not much I can do without a working voice and no other means of communication.

"I'm your speech therapist. I'm going to help you get your voice back, so to speak, and I'll also help you eat your favorite foods again." I think of my favorite foods— oatmeal, bananas, frozen entrees—and realize that they are no longer my favorites. In fact, thinking about them makes me sick.

Jenny looks at me expectantly. I try to offer a smile. I'm not sure if it worked.

"Okay. Well, some of the things I will ask you to do may seem strange, and they will be a little challenging, but we will get that beautiful mouth moving again soon. First, I need to see where we're at."

Jenny has me move my tongue around and try to make different sounds. She writes feverishly in her notepad. She is patient with my slow movements. My head aches, and I start to feel a little cranky. My eyes feel heavy.

"Are you getting tired, Amy? I just have a few more things for you to do, and then you can rest."

She gives more commands, but I no longer understand them. Sleep is pulling me back into its clutches.

"Alright, I guess that's it for now. Don't worry, it's normal to be sleepy like this after a head trauma. It will get better with time."

***

I wake again to early afternoon light. Is it the same day? A woman walks in. She is familiar.

"Hello, it's me, Heidi. How are you today, Amy?"

Doing great. Never been better. I'm glad my sarcasm is intact, but it's too bad I can't share that with her. I think she's one of the therapists that makes me move.

"It's time for your workout. We'll build your muscles back up and keep you beautiful for the guys." She winks at me. Men are the least of my concern.

She moves my right leg and asks me to push against her. I can barely do it. Then she tortures me by doing the same thing on my left leg.

My arms are much stronger than my legs. At least some part of me almost works.

"Whoo girl, you've got power in these arms. That's good news. Let's use those arms to sit you up for a minute."

Heidi is strong. She gets behind me and shows me how to use my arms—with her help—to hold the rest of my body in a sitting position. It's hard to believe that sitting up could be so exciting, but it is. It feels like freedom.

"Look who's up," says a deep voice behind us. I want to look, but I'm sure I would fall over. Tommy comes into view. His face looks flushed. "Great job, Amy."

I stare at him wondering why he's here but thankful that at least someone visits me. My arms begin to shake, and Heidi slowly guides me down into my bed. "Would you like the bed tilted up while you visit?" she asks. I nod. Heidi adjusts the bed.

Tommy sits back in his chair, beaming at me. "You're doing really great. You should be pleased with yourself. This is hard stuff, recovering from what you've been through."

I'm too tired to try to communicate, especially after I heard my voice earlier, so I lean my head back and rest. Tommy pulls something out of a bag. He hands me a notebook and a pen.

"I know you'll be talking soon, but until then, if you need to tell me something, maybe you could use this."

I look at the book. It takes a moment to realize what he means. I slowly open the notepad and scratch out the word: Thanks. I don't recognize my own handwriting.

Tommy looks at the note and says, "You're welcome. I'm glad to help any way that I can."

A startling thought pops in my head. "My cat is dead," I write. My first thought should have been for poor Fluffers. What kind of friend am I?

Tommy smiles at me. I'm not sure that should be his response.

"Your cat isn't dead. I've been feeding it."

I scratch another word. "Fluffers."

"Yes, Fluffers. I'm feeding him. Don't worry."

The notebook feels heavy in my hand. My body tingles with the desire for sleep. I try to fight, but I am powerless, and I drift to sleep again.

***

It is dark for a hospital and quiet. The ever-bustling hallway is calm. It must be the middle of the night. No one is here in my room. I let my mind wander.

I wonder if other people have had vivid, week-long dreams while in a coma. Was that what I'd had? It seemed so real, and I remember it in great detail. I remember it more than I remember the weeks before the accident. I don't know what it all means. Is my father really dead? Somehow I think that part is true, but I doubt that I really saw him or…Mom. Did I see her?

I guess I should be thankful that I'm not losing my mind.

What were all the other hallucinations about? Were they random subconscious bits of life quilted together into a haze of realistic nonsense? Maybe they'd felt so powerful because I was supposed to learn something from them, but what? That life can be scary? I already knew that. It can be awful and unfair? Knew that too. But what about love? What did it all have to say about that? Is it worth the risk?

My mind swims in vast, unanswered questions. I wish the answers were as easy to find as the questions.

{9}

Love

Many days have passed by in glimpses. It's hard to keep track of time when you sleep throughout the day like a cat. I'm awake more of the day now, but I still need lots of naps. Sleep is my most faithful friend.

I'm not sure how many days I've been in the hospital—long enough to have switched floors. The same therapists come around. Jenny has untangled my mouth so I can talk and eat. It wasn't easy, none of it is. I still slur like a drunk sometimes, and I'm not ready for chewy foods. Like a baby, I moved from pureed foods on up to things with more texture. I remember when they brought me oatmeal and a banana—my old favorites. I didn't have the ability to tell them why I found it so offensive—heck, I didn't understand it myself—but that's a part of my life that I *don't* want back. I screamed "No oatmeal" until someone removed it from the room. They brought me grits instead.

Thanks to Heidi and her team, I'm moving around better. My arms are pretty strong, but my legs lag behind. They tell me that it's not permanent, but it will take time to regain full function. It could be much worse, I'm told.

Everyone keeps telling me I'm lucky, but I don't feel like it.

Tommy visits most days. It's strange because in some ways he's comfortable, like an old sweatshirt, but other times this comfort makes me anxious. I know his affection is not likely to last, and I don't want to become dependent on him. I have no idea why he visits so often. I know he had a thing for me before, but whatever delusion he was under has to have been shattered when he listened to my sloppy voice and watched me drip food on my face. I mean, no one is that good.

***

Outside my door I hear Tommy's enthusiastic greeting to the nurses. My heartbeat quickens a bit, and I try to tell it to stop. It doesn't listen.

"Hello beautiful," Tommy says as he situates himself in his usual chair.

I am happy to see him, but I feel suspicious. Something is not adding up for me. I have to ask the question that's been on my mind since I awoke.

"Whyy ur ew ear?"

"Why am I here?" Tommy repeats. I nod. It's a system we've come up with to make sure he understands what I'm saying.

"We're friends. I know you were upset with me before…*this*…happened, but I want to be here for you. I care about you. After your accident, we tried to contact other people for you—it was a miracle that your phone was only cracked—but the only person we found was your father. We talked to his nurses and they said he…well…he couldn't come. I know what it's like to be alone, Amy. I don't want that for you, so I'm here."

"Dahd?" I want to know about my father.

I see the truth in Tommy's sad eyes.

"Deead."

Tommy stares at me for a long moment. "You mean is your father dead?"

"Yesh," I say.

"I'm sorry, he is. He passed while you were in a coma. But, how did you know that?"

I shrug. I don't have the ability to say the words to explain how I know. I'm not even sure how I know. Maybe I overheard a conversation or something and integrated it into my coma dream.

"I'm sorry about your dad," Tommy says.

He puts his hand on mine. I turn my hand over and hold his. It's is warm and reassuring.

I know now that all those experiences I'd had were not hallucinations but some sort of dream. I know they weren't real. I do hope that on some level my dad's spirit knows that I forgive him. I see now that I was being selfish. After all, he did the best he could under the circumstances.

It makes sense that I would have dreamt of him, but where had the other people in my dreams come from? The other encounters swirl in my mind—the evil rapist, the loving mother, the lustful lover, Gertrude's enduring love, and Adrienne's friendship. What were those about? Where did they come from, and what, if anything, do they mean?

***

Tommy arrives for our evening walking date. This will be our fifth one. He expertly stands the walker in front of me, just as the nurses taught him, and with a little effort, I stand. Then I shuffle my sluggish feet one in front of the other. A one-year-old could probably walk better, but it's still exciting to me to stand and drag my feet forward.

"Was it a good day at the spa?"

Tommy apparently thinks this is hilarious. I smile for him although I'm tired of this recurring joke.

"Yes, they gave me top-notch treatment. I did get some news today."

"Good news, I hope."

"Next week sometime I'm going to be moved to the rehabilitation center."

"That is great news."

"It is. It means things are moving forward. I don't think I could ask for much more."

"We'll have to celebrate."

"I don't know if I'm up for champagne yet."

"No, but we'll think of something."

I walk all the way to the nurses' station, which is about fourteen feet away from my room. I feel like I've run a marathon. We stop so I can catch my breath before the walk back. It's nice to not have to walk alone.

We walk back toward the room. I'm running out of steam.

"I know it's not fun being in the hospital, but at least you'll miss tax season this year. It's been crazy around the office. People are stressed out. We have too many clients and not enough time."

Tommy talks a lot when I'm ready to give up. I think it's his way of distracting me.

I keep trudging forward as he talks about office life. I no longer hear the specific words, only the sound of his voice, but it's enough. I reach my bed and sit like I haven't sat for days. My muscles celebrate.

I lean back and Tommy reads to me from a magazine. He reads me a story about space probes zooming through the sky. It sounds interesting and I want to listen, but my mind zones out. I'm exhausted. I watch him read. His brown eyes are warm and expressive. His masculine cheekbones and beard stubble make me want to reach out and touch his face. I want to know what it feels like. His dark brown hair is tousled, but in a good way. I watch his lips move, and I want to touch them, too. He makes a joke. I smile. I have no idea what he said, but I do know that Tommy is handsome and kind.

I listen to Tommy read more. Suddenly, he stops. I open my eyes, and he's staring at me. His eyes send me some kind of message, but I don't know exactly what it means.

"Well, it looks like it's bedtime. I'd better let you get some sleep," he says.

"Thanks," I say.

"You don't have to thank me. I love reading to you."

"Thanks for...everything. You've been a good friend, a better friend than I deserve."

He stands up and leans his tall body toward me. He puts his warm hand on my arm and says, "You are very welcome." Tommy leans over further and kisses my cheek. I'm not sure if I want him to do that. I'm about to say so when he smiles and walks away.

***

The next day, Tommy walks in after I finish my breakfast. It must be the weekend since he's here so early.

He stands in the hallway speaking with Jill, a young nurse with short blonde hair, beautiful blue eyes, and boobs that I'm sure all men notice. I don't like the way Tommy smiles at her or how she tilts her head in a flirty way. My body tenses up. I feel like I want to fight. What the hell are they talking about to make them look so happy. I'm not sure if Tommy's mine—or if I even want him—but she *certainly* can't have him!

He walks in and sits next to my bed. I can't help it. I'm annoyed.

"Don't you have to be at work?" I ask. I can feel the scowl on my face, and I don't try to hide it.

"It's Saturday," he answers.

"What are you talking with *her* for?" As I hear the words exit my mouth, I know they are vicious and pathetic.

Tommy laughs. I don't see what's so damn funny. He places his warm hand on my hand. I feel him looking at me, but I look away.

"What's so funny?" I sneer.

"You'd better be careful, Amy Clark. If I didn't know better, I'd think you're jealous. Am I finally growing on you?"

I think about that for a moment. Tommy *is* kind of growing on me. I can't deny that I have feelings for him, but they feel dangerous, like they could whip around and stab me in the heart. It's complicated. There are things inside me I don't quite understand.

"No reason for jealousy, if that's what it was. I only have eyes for you," Tommy says. "I was asking Jill if you could come on a little field trip with me."

"First of all, I'm not jealous." I turn to look at him. "Second, what kind of field trip?"

"Well, when I first started visiting you, some of the nurses felt bad for me as I pined for you during your beauty sleep." He gives me his contagious smile. "Trying to distract me from my anguish, they convinced me to volunteer on the pediatric floor. I go there a couple of times each week to read to the kids and get my mind off the girl that I *do* like." He smiles at me expectantly. "So, since you're leaving here in a few days, I thought you might want to come with me and see it. The nurses said they are okay with that, as long as we keep the visit brief. What do you say? Would you like to look at something besides these walls?" He gestures toward the walls.

"Actually, I would. I feel like I've been trapped in this place for years."

"Great. Jill is ordering some wheels for you, and when they get here, we'll be off."

Nurse Jill comes in. I thank her, even though I'm annoyed with her flirting ways and large chest. She tells me the rules. I'm supposed to stay in the chair, and if I feel strange or sick I'm to come back immediately. I'm sure that I'll be fine. I've been getting steadily better every day. That's why they're sending me to rehab.

I feel giddy. I hadn't realized how oppressive these walls had become until I think of leaving them.

The wheelchair arrives. It could be a limousine the way I feel right now. Tommy holds it steady while I situate myself in it. I wish that I didn't need it, but I guess I should be thankful that one day I won't.

Tommy steers me down the hall, and we travel by elevator to the main floor. My stomach lurches on the downward journey.

Tommy says, "This is the long way, but I thought you might want to take a look around. Don't tell anyone." He wheels me into a large open area that is filled with round dining tables. The lunch area is surrounded by small stores, restaurants, and a café. Large windows on one wall brighten the space with natural light. Cushiony leather chairs and couches sit in groups in front of the windows. Tall plants dot the entire floor. I touch one as we pass it. It's real. I've never seen this part of the hospital. It's much nicer than I expected. I haven't been in a hospital since saying goodbye to my mother all those years ago. I push the thought aside.

"Would you like a coffee before we head to the pediatric floor?"

"Yes, I would. Thanks."

I watch Tommy stroll over to the small café. I notice that his jeans fit nicely over his behind. My face flushes warm.

He walks back to me, a coffee in each hand, and sits down. He hands me my drink and lifts his in a toast. "To coffee. I need to be caffeinated to put on my best performance."

"What's it like there? Isn't it sad?"

"Yes, it is…a little. But once you get past the idea that these are really sick kids and see them for just kids, it's cool. They really appreciate visits. I've been reading them this." He lifts up a Junie B. Jones book. "They seem to really like it. I've never done anything like this in my whole life, but it's a great feeling."

"You're a good guy. I mean you read to sick kids, you've been here for me, you're almost too good to be true."

"Well, I'm here for my own reasons too. I figured this was my window to get you to finally notice me."

I look up from my coffee and give him a play frown. I don't know what to say. I can't believe he still likes me. Why would he?

"Whoa, don't get mad. It's a joke! A joke! Well, not really." He laughs again.

"It's fine. I'm thankful you're here. Whatever your reasons." I smile at him. My cheeks start to burn again. Why are they doing that?

We drink our coffee and watch people walk to the restaurants and shops, taking a break from the business of hospitals. We throw our empty cups in the trash, and Tommy pushes me to the east side elevators. The elevator whisks us up to the eighth floor. My heart drops. It must be the elevator.

We zigzag through a labyrinth of halls to get to the children's hospital wing. Tommy checks in at the nurses' station. A few of the female nurses welcome him too warmly for my taste. They inform me that they are re-sponsible for me while I'm on their floor and to tell them if I have any problems.

As we walk down the hall, I notice how small the bod-ies are lying in the hospital beds. It makes me cringe to think of kids enduring long hospital stays and sickness.

Tommy pushes my chair into a room labeled the Rec Room.

"Hi Tommy," says an overly cheerful man.

"Hey, Travis. How are things with you?"

"Good. It's good to see you again. I see you brought a visitor." Travis looks at me.

"Yes, may I introduce you to Amy."

"Good to finally meet you. Tommy has told us about his sleeping beauty. We're so glad that you're awake. It's an inspirational story to these kids." Travis turns to Tom-my. "Well, the kids are almost ready for you. The rest of them should be down soon." With that he smiles and walks across the room.

I'm not sure what I expected, but this is not it. The room is so cheerful that even a kid who isn't sick would want to be here. The walls of the large room are painted a bright, inviting blue. Cushioned chairs of different sizes and colors wrap around a table shaped like a giant kidney bean. A large, flat-screen TV is attached to a wall. On the other side of the room is a foosball table, a shelf stacked with board games, a table with drawing supplies, and next to that, easels. Small chairs are lined up in the middle of the room. Are those for Tommy's audience? Two young boys with bald heads sit near the front. A girl in a wheel-chair rolls in. Tommy speaks with each of them.

"Hey Joe and Bill. What's up? Anna, nice to see you."

"Hi Mr. Tommy," they say in unison.

"Are you reading Junie B. today? Can we read some of these Silverstein poems? My mom just bought this for me." Joe hands Tommy a white book.

"Sure."

Other children walk or wheel in over the next few minutes, and Tommy chats with each one.

"I think we're ready to start. First, I want to introduce my friend Amy," says Tommy.

"Is she the one who woke up?" asks a girl.

"Yes, the one and only."

"Is she your girlfriend?" asks Bill.

"No. We're just friends," Tommy says. The boys laugh. Tommy gives me a warm smile.

"Let's see..." Tommy thumbs through some pages of the book. "Where were we? Ah-ha, here we are." He begins to read. I watch the children. They are fidgety at first. Then I notice that one by one they find a comfortable position, settle in, and listen. Some of them look at Tommy with affection.

How did it happen that before I was in a coma, I had no one. And now I seem to have Tommy? How is it that I like having him, too? Why would he choose to stand by my side when we barely even know each other? I wasn't exactly Ms. Sweet to him before the accident, either.

My eyes grow heavy as I listen to the story. I will myself to stay awake. All this recovery makes me so tired.

Tommy stands up. "Now for some poetry." He picks up the poem book. He stands as he reads and becomes animated. The kids laugh at his enthusiasm. Behind him the door opens and a girl enters in a wheelchair that is pushed by a man. The top of her head is wrapped with bandages. Long blonde hair sticks out of the bottom of the bandage near her neck. She seems familiar. But why? The man wheels the girl to an open spot next to me.

Tommy stops reading. "I don't believe we've met," he says. "My name is Tommy. What's your name?"

The girl looks up. She has vivid blue eyes. I know those eyes.

"My name's Adrienne," says the little girl.

"Nice to meet you, Adrienne. We were just reading some funny poems. Would you like to stay and listen?"

"Okay."

My pulse quickens. Panic charges through my body. How can it be? I can't stop staring at the little girl. I want Adrienne to look at me and tell me if she remembers me. The man looks over at me. I must look like a lunatic. I look away.

It doesn't make sense. How can this be? My chest feels tight. I break into a sweat—I feel it on my upper lip and wipe it away. I try to look away from Adrienne, but I can't help but keep looking back. I do not hear a word of what Tommy's reading, but I hear his voice. The children start shifting and moving around the room. Tommy isn't reading anymore. When did he stop? He stands with the book closed in front of him. A look of concern crosses his face as he looks at me.

He turns back to the children. "Good to see all of you. Tomorrow's Sunday, so I'll be back for another reading. Tune in to see what happens next."

I turn toward Adrienne again. She looks back at me. Her escort walks away to chat with Tommy.

"Hi," I say.

"Hi," Adrienne says.

"Have we met before?" I ask her.

"No. I don't think so. But I don't remember everything right now. I don't think we've met. Have we?"

"No, probably not," I answer. "You just look like someone I know."

"Oh."

It is her, without a doubt. "Well, have a good...see you—"

I need to leave. I push against the chair's wheels, but they are locked. I fumble with the lock and start pushing myself toward the door.

Tommy rushes over. "Hey, what's your hurry?"

"I'm just...tired. I need to get back."

"You look a little pale. Are you okay?"

"Yeah, I'm just really tired."

"Okay, let me help you."

He pushes me down the corridor, away from the pediatric hall. My pulse rushes in my ears. I hold my hands together tightly to hide the shaking. If Adrienne is a real person, what does it mean for me? I thought all those people were figments of my coma dream. If they're not, then what the hell does it mean? It doesn't make any sense.

Goosebumps rise on my skin. I rub my hands over my arms to create warmth. Everything passes in a baffling blur. When we are inside the elevator, Tommy stops to look at me.

"Are you okay, Amy?"

"Yes, I just feel a little dizzy. I need to rest."

"We'll take a short cut, okay? We can go down this hall and it'll take us to the west side faster. Don't tell anyone," Tommy smiles, but I see the concern in his eyes.

He wheels me down a floor that looks much like mine. I can't tell what type of floor it is because the words dance in front of my unfocused eyes.

A familiar voice yells, "Georgy, look out!" I don't want to look up. I have this sense of impending doom. A boy runs in front of my chair and Tommy stops quickly. I look up and see the woman from the post office scolding her son. "You can't run out in front of people!" Her head is bandaged and she's wearing a hospital gown with a robe over it. The woman leans on her walker, looks me in the eye, and says, "Sorry. It's hard to keep track of these little guys."

My face is stiff like stone. My eyes don't leave the woman until Tommy pushes me past her.

I hear a thud. Tommy reaches down to pick up his book. He hands it to me to carry. My hands shake as I reach for it. I look away from Tommy. I don't want him to see me undone. It takes every ounce of will I have not to scream and cry.

"Everything okay?" Tommy asks.

"Will you please stop asking me that?" My lips move but my jaw is clamped shut.

Tommy's face moves to the side as if he's been slapped.

"Okay, let's get you back." He pushes me wordlessly through the corridor.

An attendant pushes a hospital bed through an open elevator door. He nearly hits my chair with it. "Sorry," he says. The jolt of the fast swerve to the left makes me look up at the man lying on the bed. His white face lacks color but for a large healing gash on the side of his face. He lifts his head up and smiles at me despite his grotesque condition.

It is the man from the grocery store. He looks at me in an appraising manner like he did the first time that I saw him. Bile rises in my throat. I begin to dry heave. My God. Make it stop!

Tommy runs to the nearest nurses' station. He comes back with a vomit bag. I hold it over my mouth. My heaves don't produce anything. My mind reels. My head begins to pound. It feels like my brain is growing too large for my skull.

"Get me out of here, Tommy. I need to get back to my room."

Tommy pushes me down another hall and we near my room door. He stops in front of the nurses' station.

"She turned pale and nearly vomited. You've got to look at her."

Nurse Jill tries to talk to me. I want to respond, but my mouth is disconnected from my mind. All I can think about is that man's face. I can't erase the visual. I try to open my mouth again, but it is shut tight. I don't know what I would say even if I could open it. The room spins around and around. Tears start to stream down my face as Tommy and the nurse help me into bed. I try to talk again; this time garbled nonsense babbles from my mouth. I lay, feigning tiredness, mind racing. The nurse gives me a pill.

I try to hide my downward spiral, but I can't communicate with anyone. I know Tommy is watching me, worried, but I have no comfort to give. I lay there for long moments until merciful peace comes through sleep.

**

I wake up crying. I feel like I never slept, but according to the clock, it is morning. I am hopeless. Why did I wake up, only to be fucking nuts? Why did I have that pointless, hopeful moment? Why did I think maybe I could glean a normal life after the accident? I actually thought that it was like a second chance or something. I thought I had a shot at happiness. Of course that bullshit is only in fairytales and movies. It just isn't real. Cruelty, pain. Now those things are real. I should have known better than to change my ways. Tommy won't want me now. No one will. Now I will have truly nothing—no work, no family, no one to care for a broken, crazy woman.

I should have stuck with my original life plan. Life is easier when you're alone. There's no anxiety about hurting other people, or worse, being hurt by them.

I hear Tommy greet the nurses in the hallway. He walks into my room. He smells of the outdoors, of forest and trees.

"Hello beautiful," he says, seating himself next to me. "How are you feeling?"

I stare at him. I am so numb that my face is expressionless. Talking is senseless at this point. He needs to leave and never come back. He must save himself. He's too nice for this madness.

"Not talkative. I see. Did you just wake up?"

Nothing.

He leaves the room and speaks with one of the nurses. He comes back into the room. He will not give up easily. It must be a clean break. This will be hard, but maybe this is the *one* good thing I can do in my life—save Tommy.

I stare ahead. I'm trying to build my strength up for a good performance. I cannot cry. I must be convincing.

Tommy sits carefully on the side of my bed. I turn my head in the other direction.

"What's going on? Did I do something wrong?" The concern in his voice makes sadness bubble up within me. I don't want to hurt him, but I have to. It's hard enough knowing I'll be in a straightjacket soon. I don't want to ruin him too. I'm not sure what to say, so I remain silent.

"Okay, I get the point. You need some alone time. That's fine. All you had to do was say so." He sighs deeply. "I'll go get some lunch and then come back. Do you need anything?"

"Don't." The pain of all that had happened since my accident doesn't compare to the pain of what I am about to do. The right thing to do, the only thing, is to let Tommy go. He deserves better.

"Okay, you don't want anything. I'll be back." Tommy stands to leave.

"Don't," I command.

"Don't what?" he asks.

"Don't bother coming back." I know that I have to push him hard to stay away. I can't have him coming back. It will be too painful. "Thanks for helping me out, but don't come back. I never asked you to be there for me. I told you long ago that I wasn't interested in a relationship. This has gone on too long. Get back to your own life."

"I...Why are you doing this? I thought we were—"

"I don't want you here. Not now, not ever. Don't you get it?" I look away. I don't want him to see the tears burning my eyes.

"I get it now." I can't help but look at him. He looks down, his lips set in a firm line. "Goodbye."

***

I sit there for many hours stewing in what I have done. Of course, I have no visitors, except nurses, to make the time go by faster. I guess it's time to get used to being alone again. It is what I created. I know it's for the best, but it doesn't make it hurt any less.

Jill disrupts my descent into self-pity. "How are you doing?"

"Couldn't be better," I answer sarcastically.

"Good. Good to hear that." She gives me a knowing smile. "What, no boyfriend tonight?"

"He's not my boyfriend."

"Oh, I see. Well, good news. You're officially out of here. You are scheduled to move to rehab tomorrow. It shouldn't be too long there; you're doing incredibly well."

I had been looking forward to this news, but now I wonder, what's the point? I feel Jill's eyes on me.

"You might want to call and let your *friend* know where you'll be if he's not coming tonight."

"Who I call is none of your business."

Jill's holds her lips tight together and breathes deeply.

"Tomorrow's my day off, so I won't see you before you leave. Best of luck to ya." And with that she walks toward the door. She pauses, turns back, and says, "You know, good guys don't come around too often. Don't give that nice boy too hard of a time. It's obvious he's crazy about you."

Like I need a reminder.

{10}

Acceptance

"Good morning, Amy," the physical therapist, Kim, says in her sing-song voice. What does this woman have to be so happy about? She has woken me up with this cheery voice many times over the weeks I've been at rehab.

"Morning."

"Look outside. The sun is shining. It's a great day to get your exercise on. You ready to do your Jane Fonda?" She thinks this joke is funny, but it's old. I want to say mean things to her cheerfulness, but somehow I just can't. I've hurt enough people, so I shut my mouth.

We walk down the hall together to the exercise room where she puts me through another round of physical hell. I welcome it though, because the therapies required to rehabilitate my body make time move forward at breakneck speed. The time between waking up and lunch feels like one long, painful minute. I've had many of these. That may sound bad, but the rest of my time is worse. Time makes up for those fast bursts by cruelly slowing to a snail's pace, giving me more time to miss Tommy and fear more hallucinations. Sometimes minutes stretch into what feels like days.

When I'm not busy putting my body through the wringer or dabbling in depression, I sleep. Sleep used to be a peaceful getaway that took away my problems, but something has changed. My dreams have grown vivid, real, and frightening. I wake in the night with soaked sheets and shaking hands.

Some parts of my dreams are only strange. Like my father...he's often camouflaged among the furniture of my dreams. He is literally part of the backdrop somewhere, then he pops out suddenly, and says strange things that make no sense, like, "You can't lose if you don't play," or "You can't play hide-and-seek from what you see." For not having had much to say when he was alive, he sure makes up for it now.

Last night I dreamt of the grocery store man. He chased me through the aisles, pulling at my pants when he caught up to me. I grabbed the bottom can of soup from a towering store display so the rest would come tumbling behind. The man was pulverized by the falling cans and transformed into specks of darkness, which turned to oily slime on the linoleum floor. I put my hands on my knees and struggled to catch my dream breath.

When I stood to look around, no one else was there. I walked through the abandoned store. The automatic doors closed behind me as I stood in the empty parking lot, looking across the street at a bar with another empty parking lot. Not a single car or person passed by on the main drag of my small hometown, or anywhere else for that matter. I knew that if I walked in any direction, I'd find the same thing –complete emptiness.

The strangest part was that when I woke up, I looked around and thought the hospital was empty too. I didn't hear any sounds of equipment or nurses. I was terrified. I lay there in the quiet morning until the buzz of activity started again.

"Earth to Amy," Kim says. I'm sitting on an exercise machine in a daze. This happens to me lately. My mind wanders. "Let's do five more. Come on, you can do it." Kim pushes me hard to do a few more reps, as she does every day. She paints a smile on her face and puts up with my attitude. If I had any kindness left to give, I'd give her some. I should be thankful—I am walking and nearly strong enough to leave this place thanks to her and her assistants. But then I wonder…why? What's the point? I have nothing to go back to. I don't even have my comfortable habits any longer. My mindless routines don't fulfill me the way they used to. I don't eat the same foods anymore, I don't time my showers, and I don't do things in precise segments. Reminders of that self repulse me.

And what happens when I get back home? Will the hallucinations start again? Then what do I do? Where will I work? I don't think I can go back to Douglas Accounting. I can't face Tommy every day, or any day for that matter.

***

I now know what bittersweet really means. I wake from an afternoon nap and my insides are electrified from my dream. Tommy and I shared a steamy kiss in my slumber.

I didn't know that a kiss could do so much, but just imagining it makes my heart jolt and my body perspire. If I had a choice, I would stay in that dream, even though I know every minute it lasts makes the reality of my situation much worse. Tommy and I are done. He was the first man to show me romantic love and the last.

Any chance I had of love vanished with those hallucinations. The ironic part is that the hallucinations, or whatever they were, made me realize what I was missing in the first place. I would have stayed alone my whole life and been okay with it. I'll still be alone my whole life but I've been shown this other way…the possibility and potential of love with no hope of ever having it. All hope dried up the day I saw the people who I thought I had only dreamt about. Or, at least I thought I saw them. They were probably only hallucinations. Who knows what is real anymore. Clearly I don't.

I amble to the bathroom. I scrub my face like crazy can be washed off. I slowly lumber down the hallway (all my walks are slow these days). It uplifts me a little to leave my room. I feel like it's suffocating me. At this place, if you're able to walk, they encourage you to go to the little cafeteria. I don't need to be asked twice. I choose a dinner option and they bring it to me. I try a new kind of pasta with olive oil and sundried tomatoes. The taste bursts in my mouth. It is delicious.

Before I walk back to my room, I take a look out the tall windows overlooking a garden. Fat spring peony buds sit atop their stems. They will open soon. I will be out of here in days. What will happen to me then?

I watch the nurses with a patient that I haven't seen before. The woman stands behind her walker and shuffles slowly down the hallway away from me. I used to be like her. Now, I'm nearly healed, at least in body. The woman's dark brown hair looks familiar. Then I notice a man walking down the hall. My face blushes without asking permission. It's the man that had made love to me—or to Jenna, the woman I met in the bar. I think his name is David. He places his hand gently on her back as she struggles to make it down the hall. It's such a small gesture, his hand, but somehow his movement brims with love.

What happened to Jenna? How did she go from waiting for her boyfriend at the bar, to rehab? It's possible that I never even saw her at the bar. Is she really here now or is she only a figment of my illness?

My feet are rooted to the floor, but my veins feel like they could pump blood out of my skin. I can't run, so I stare.

A nurse walks toward me and pauses. "Are you okay?" he asks.

"Yes, I um. Do you see that woman down the hall?" Hopefully there really is a person down there or I might have outed my problems.

"The one with the walker?"

I nod, relief floods through me. "I think I know that woman."

"Well you should have a chat with her. Maybe not right now, it looks like she's having a rough time, but later or tomorrow. In here, people can use all the company they can get. Am I right? Recovery is hard work."

I stare at him. Obviously, he doesn't know he's talking with someone who hasn't had a single visitor, but I'll forgive him.

"Okay," is all I can muster.

Maybe I will. I don't *want* to face her, I worry what will happen if I do, but hasn't the worst already happened? I mean, what if she remembers me? What if somehow I can understand something about what's happened? If she is a real person, if the nurse can see her too, how can it be a hallucination?

Too many questions. My mind is spinning. It makes me dizzy. I carefully make my way back to my room and ground myself to the bed. I lean back and let the questions run through my mind, hoping they'll tire themselves out and let peaceful sleep come my way. They don't; it doesn't.

***

The early sun peeking through the curtains wakes me. It seems like I've been awake all night, but I must have slept at some point. I'm determined to have a conversation with Jenna today. I'm terrified, but determined. What is the worst that could happen?

PT calls, with Kim's smiling, over-cheerful face. On the way to PT, I notice the location of Jenna's room. I don't know what I'll say to her, but I need to find out if she remembers me. Therapy doesn't go by as quickly today as it usually does. I'm too keyed-up thinking about the conversation to come.

Working my body hard requires some rest, even if my mind is impatient. I take an hour of down time, and then I'm off to see if I can find any answers. I trek down the hall to Jenna's room. She's having a snack in bed. Her boyfriend isn't around, thank goodness, so I knock.

"Hello, do you mind if I come in? I'm a neighbor from down the hall."

"Come on in," she calls back.

"Hello." I'm nearly struck speechless looking at her face. Part of her beautiful hair has been shaved, but it is her, without a doubt.

"Hello." She looks at me expectantly.

"Sorry to bother you..."

"This place is boring; you're not a bother. I'm glad for a distraction, believe me."

"Well, good. I'm Amy. I'm not sure, but I think we might have met before. You look so...familiar. Do you remember me?"

"Hmmm, I have to say, it's hard to remember things right now. See, I had a stroke, and it's done some terrible things to my brain and my memory. I even forgot how to walk it seems."

"I'm sorry to hear that. I didn't know young people had those. You look so young."

"Thanks, I'm close to thirty. I was surprised too, to say the least! I've forgotten a lot of things, it's possible we do know each other and I just don't remember. I'm just not sure." She stares at me. "Although I think I'd remember if I met you, with those bright blue eyes. They don't seem like something you'd forget."

"Thanks. Well maybe I'm mistaken. Maybe you just remind me of someone. I can't be sure. I'm sorry to hear about your stroke. I hope you recover quickly." I stand up to leave.

"You don't have to leave, unless you've got better things to do. Want to stay and hang out for a while?"

"Oh, okay." I sit back down, wondering what we could talk about. I can't tell her anything that I'm *really* thinking.

We sit watching the home improvement show that plays on the television.

"I mean one minute I was sitting there waiting for David, and the next, I was out cold. That's what they tell me anyway."

It feels like she's continuing a conversation that never started, but I go with it. "That is something. Who are 'they'?"

"The people at the bar."

The bar? "The one in Roscommon?" Oops, that probably sounded weird, but it blurted out.

"No. Where's Roscommon?"

"It's in Michigan. Sorry, I don't know why I even said that."

"I haven't spent much time in Michigan. No, I was at The Roadhouse Pub, on the north side, close to where I live. It's a watering hole not far from my apartment. I was waiting for my boyfriend. He works late hours. Anyway, I'm glad I wasn't waiting at my apartment. They say the quick response is what helped things work out all right."

"Well, that's good. That's good it all worked out all right."

"Yes, I'm more than thankful. I'm not ready to go yet, if you know what I'm saying. This is going to suck for a while, maybe a long while, but it's better than the alternative. At least at this point."

"You're right." I nod my head. I don't know how to respond.

"Listen to me drumming on about myself. What about you? What are you in for?" She smiles at her joke.

"I was hit by a car. I was in a coma for a while, and I'm still figuring out how to use my legs. It's gotten a lot better though. I'll be going home soon. They said maybe a day or two."

"That is good news. I'm happy to hear that. I see that you're a lucky girl too."

"What do you mean?" Lucky is not at all what I'd consider myself to be.

"Well, we both could have died, but we didn't. The way I see it, that's a gift. It's a gift I'm happy to have."

"That's a good way to look at it. I haven't thought about it that way."

***

I wait in the rehab lobby for my cab. I feel like a prisoner being released to the outside, except I don't feel free, and I don't want to go. I don't remember how to do "normal" life, and I don't want to go back to my pre-coma normal anyway. What else is there, then? It's too confusing.

The cab drops me off in front of my building. I'm instantly reminded of Fluffers. I wonder if Tommy is still feeding him. He doesn't seem the type to let a cat die, but I still worry.

The walk to the elevator is laborious. It takes way too long to get there, but at least I can do it, I guess. I push the button for the eighth floor. My feet tingle. I lumber to my apartment. I slow down because my legs threaten to give out. I open the door. It all looks the same, but it is different. Maybe I'm different. Fluffers greets me by rubbing urgently on my leg. I reach down and pick up my old friend. The tears fall freely for all that I've lost. Fluffers purrs on.

There is a note in the entryway. It says,

Amy, I've been feeding Fluffers. Please let me know when you're back home so I don't come over. I hope you're well.
—Tommy

"Well, Fluffers, I'll have to call Tommy. Thank goodness you're okay, old friend." My phone is cracked and barely functioning. I decide I'll call or text him in the morning. It's been a full day, and I can't deal with that right now.

My apartment hasn't changed one bit. I no longer find its sparseness comforting. It is cold and needs to change. I don't know how, but it does. I look in the fridge. It's pretty empty. I look in the cupboards. They are filled with little but oatmeal. My freezer has ample amounts of frozen food. No more. I rip the oatmeal out of the cupboard and the frozen meals from the freezer and throw them in the garbage. I don't know what I'll eat, but I won't eat these things. I'd rather starve.

I look at the food piled in the garbage and it makes me hungry. I dial up a Chinese restaurant and order food I've never eaten before. I sit with Fluffers and wait for my delivery. I look out at the buildings across the road. I wonder what the people behind those windows are doing. Are they enjoying life? Are they hurting the people they supposedly love? Thinking about so many lives occurring simultaneously makes my brain hurt. I hope they are living lives like Jenna's or Gertrude's. I hope the world has more good in it than I used to think. I can't bear to focus on the bad anymore. I can't live waiting for the next calamity. I don't know how to be a positive or good person, but I have to change. If I continue this way, I'll wither away; I'll do nothing but add bitterness to the world. I don't want that life anymore. That's the only thing that I know with certainty.

The Chinese food finally comes, and I devour it. I stand over the counter, shoving food into my mouth like a staving person. I never eat like that. But it feels and tastes good. Salty, but good.

Fluffers stares at this new ferocious eating mystery I've become. Then, after I sit down on the couch, he plops his warm little body on my lap, and his purring continues into my sleep, as do my thoughts.

***

I text Tommy in the morning:

> I'm home, no need to feed Fluffers. Thanks so much for doing it!

He kept my cat alive. I think I should get him a gift or something as a thank you. I don't want him back or anything, if I ever had him, but a proper thanks is in order. I call in a work favor to get his address.

I can't decide what he might like, so I decide on a houseplant. There's a florist between his apartment and mine. He can take care of the plant now instead of Fluffers. I'll just drop it by and say a quick thanks. Anyway, it will give me something to do.

The busyness of the city shocks me. I've been in slow rehab mode for too long. I plod to the florist, which is only down the block. It's my PT for the day. Then I take a cab to Tommy's. I write on the card I purchased. The road bumps make my writing look squiggly. The note reads:

> Thanks for taking care of my cat. You are a good person. I'm sorry things didn't work out.
> Best Wishes,
> Amy

I consider leaving it with Tommy's doorman but decide he deserves face-to-face gratitude, although it will be hard. I doubt my decision the whole way up to his apartment, but my feet keep walking despite my uncertainty.

Tommy opens soon after my knock.

"Hi." My voice trembles.

"Hey," Tommy says.

I lift the plant toward him. My hands shake. "This is for you."

"Thanks," he says, taking it from me.

"I, uh, I wanted to thank you for taking care of Fluffers. Especially after...after the way I treated you. You're a good person. Thank you."

Tommy's hard stare softens. "Would you like to come in?"

"No, I should get going. I don't want to cause any trouble. I just wanted to say thanks."

"Okay, suit yourself." He squints. "You're welcome. Best of luck to you, Amy." He gives me a fake smile and slowly closes the door.

I am an asshole. What is my problem? I like this guy. He likes me. I know things could go terribly wrong. He could hate me, I could go crazy, he could break my heart... The list is endless. But, what if... What if we didn't do those things? And what if we did? Would there be good times too? Good times between the bad? I don't know what I *should* do, but I *want* to bang on his door and see what happens from there.

For many moments, I stand there, assessing risk. I take a few steps down the hall. Then, I turn around. Fuck it, I decide. I have to knock on that door, and I do.

Tommy opens the door. "Back so soon?" he asks. His smile is genuine.

"If it's all right, I would like to come in. Only if you don't mind..."

Without a word, he opens the door wider and steps aside. I walk next to him and into his apartment. It's warm, full of things to look at, and cozy.

"Would you like to sit down?" he asks as he moves toward the living room couch.

I sit down in the chair next to him. There is awkward silence. I don't know what to say. I can't even count on my voice to work. My body shakes slightly with the pulsing of my heart.

I know he's waiting for me to say something, anything. All I can think of is, "I'm really sorry."

"You don't have to be sorry. What's there to be sorry about?"

"I do have to be sorry. You don't deserve the way I treated you. You're so nice. The nicest guy I've ever met. I mean, who waits at the hospital bed of someone they barely know?"

"I want to know you, Amy. Haven't you figured that out yet?"

"I get that. And honestly, I want the same thing. I do. But I'm not...there's something wrong with my head or there was something wrong or..."

"That's what a coma does to people. You're actually doing quite—"

"That's not what I mean. I thought I was on the verge of losing my mind. I *could* be losing it." I say forcefully. The words come out before my mind realizes that I said them. Letting out my truth makes me feel nervous, relieved, and worried again about my sanity.

"I'm sure it's normal to feel that way after all you've been through."

"That's not it!" I say with firmness. He looks disappointed, like a sad puppy. I'd been right the first time; I'm not cut out for this stuff. Anyway, I don't know that the hallucinations won't come back. "Thanks for everything

Tommy. I appreciate it, I really do, but you should probably move on."

"I get it. I'm not your type. Is that what you're saying?" Tommy's jaw clenches.

I watch his Adam's apple bob up and down. How can a man's neck be so sexy? Never mind. Focus! "You would be anyone's type. It's not about you. There might be something wrong with me."

"I get it. I've heard the it's-not-you-it's-me speech before."

"No, it's not like that. I'm trying to do what's best for you here."

"What the hell do you mean, Amy? Stop talking like this and tell me what you mean."

This is getting me nowhere. Honesty seems like the only choice.

"When I was...in a coma...I saw things. Strange things."

"Like?"

"Well, I saw my dad die, for one. I was there. I saw my mother too, her ghost, probably. That's why I wasn't surprised that he had died. I already knew."

"That's—"

"Just let me finish. This isn't easy. I saw other things too. I saw people I never knew before. I didn't just see them, I became them, briefly. That alone could be a dream, but then I saw some of those people at the hospital. Remember the man on the bed with the gash on his head? We saw him right before I dry heaved. I saw him rape a woman. I saw the whole thing. It was awful." I rub my fingers against my eyes. I have to continue before I lose courage. "The woman in the hallway at the hospital...the one whose kid almost ran right in front of my wheelchair...I was somehow inside her body earlier. I felt her terror when her son ran into the street. Then, the new girl that was wheeled into the pediatrics rec room with the bandage on her head? Adrienne. I know her well. I know that she was in a car accident. Her mom was too. Her mom might have died, I'm not sure."

"How—"

"I also saw her grandmother—"

"How did you know?"

"What?"

"How did you know she was in a car accident and that her mother died?"

"Some part of my insanity, I guess. I don't understand any of it. It's not normal. That's what I'm trying to tell you. I'm probably plum-fucking crazy and you should run, Tommy."

"This is a lot to take in," he looks down at his fidgeting hands.

I should never have come, and I certainly should never have teased myself with the idea that maybe I could have a relationship. I stand up. Tommy stands up in front of me. He puts his warm hands on my shoulders.

"Something happened to you," he says.

"Clearly."

"No, listen. I went to the pediatric floor the next day. I overheard the nurses talking about that girl. She *was* in a car accident, and sadly, her mom didn't make it. They said it was a miracle that the girl lived. I guess it was touch-and-go for a while."

Hearing this is like getting slammed in the chest. I know what being motherless is like.

"Poor Adrienne."

"But *how* did you know that? You weren't there any other time, and I only heard it the next day. I never told you that."

"I know because I played with her. We talked. She told me to come out of my coma. She was at my father's funeral. She—"

"This doesn't make any sense," says Tommy.

"That's what I'm saying."

"I don't know what happened to you, but I don't think you're crazy."

"Oh, I am...I—"

"Stop, Amy. How can it mean you're crazy if the people are real?" Tommy asks.

"I don't know. It doesn't matter. It's not normal."

"What you went through must have been terrifying, but it doesn't mean there's something wrong. Maybe it's some kind of gift."

"Gift? How the hell can that—"

"I don't claim to have the answers. I don't know what it means, but I would pay attention to it."

I sigh. I don't know what it was. I don't know what any of it means. I look up at Tommy's warm eyes, his kind face. I want nothing more than to reach out to him. Why is it so hard? The heat from his hands on my shoulders flows through my body.

I have to reach out, consequences be damned.

I put my hand on his cheek. I've wanted to do that for so long. No one has ever looked at me the way he does. I pull him in for a hug. I've never felt so sure, so safe. We stand that way, holding each other tightly, for many beautiful moments.

He pulls back from me and cups my cheeks in his strong hands. He leans in slowly and kisses me. It is unlike anything I've ever felt in my whole life. My whole body, soul, and mind, are all focused on this intense, pulsating warmth. I'm not sure, but I think it might be love.

Epilogue

The bacon sizzles in the pan. The morning sun warms my back as I flip the meat. Tommy whips the eggs and pours them into a pan of sautéed onions and peppers. I love working together with him like this. Sundays mean big breakfasts at our place, and this Sunday is no exception. The smell of our breakfast permeates the air and mingles with the aroma of morning coffee.

"Would you like some oatmeal with that?" Tommy asks.

"I didn't know I'd married a comedian. Very funny," I say. I don't care if I ever see oatmeal again. He uses this joke a lot. I'm tired of it, but I keep that to myself.

I smooth my shirt over my ever-expanding belly. Earlier this morning, I felt the baby move. At first it scared me, someone else moving in my body, but then I calmed down and became more anxious to meet the girl growing inside me.

"Is she moving again?" Tommy asks, gently touching my belly. He was devastated to miss it the first time, but I'm sure there'll be many other opportunities.

"Not at the moment. I can't believe how much I'm stretching. If this is what I look like at five months, what will I look like at nine?"

"Beautiful," he says, not missing a beat.

A warm feeling enters my heart. Tears suddenly form, betraying my emotions, which I'm still not comfortable with showing.

"Hey," Tommy says, turning toward me and putting his arms around my waist. "What's wrong?"

"It's...just..." I lean in close to him, letting the tears go free. "I'm so happy," I say, crying harder.

"If this is what happy looks like, then—"

I pull back and look him in the eye. "I am happier than I've ever been. I love you so much. I feel so thankful right now." I take a deep breath and wipe away the tears. "Now, I would like to eat," I say. I want to move away from these deep emotions.

Tommy lifts his lips in a warm smile. "Let me serve you, my lady," he says as he pulls out a chair for me. I watch as Tommy expertly plates my breakfast food.

Lately, my emotions have been catching me off guard with their intensity. It must be pregnancy.

Tommy places a full plate in front of me and pours the decaffeinated coffee.

"Thank you, Tommy."

"You're welcome," he says seating himself.

"I mean, thank you for more than this breakfast. Thank you for being so wonderful."

"Well, I try," he says, smiling. Can't he ever be serious?

"I've been thinking a lot about how we got here. I mean, two years ago, I never would have guessed that I would be here with you today."

"I was hoping so, but—"

"Well, I had no idea. If...all *that*...hadn't happened, I probably *would* be eating oatmeal. *Alone.*"

"I would have won you over somehow. Don't you think?" He says as he forks food into his mouth.

"I don't know. I was pretty set in my ways."

"Well, thank goodness all of that did happen then."

"Do you ever wonder what it *was* though?" I ask.

"Of course I do. But we'll never have all the answers."

"Do you still think it might have been God?" I ask.

"I do."

"I don't know. It could have been the position of the stars, or maybe those other people were in comas and our wandering minds crossed paths, or some other unexplainable phenomenon. I'm not sure. I have a hard time believing that God would care enough about little old me to do that. I mean, it changed my life."

"How couldn't He? I mean, I adore you."

"Oh, be serious, Tommy."

"I am. I guess no matter what, you have to remember what it taught you and live life accordingly."

"You're right. I'm trying to do that. Thank goodness you stuck beside me. Most men would have sent me to the looney bin!"

"I knew you weren't crazy."

Tommy gives me a smile and starts in on more breakfast.

I guess I'll never know with certainty what happened to me. I try not to think about it too much, but when I do, I'm never sure. Sometimes I agree with Tommy and think maybe it was God. Other times, I decide it was a big hallucination of some sort, or maybe an out-of-body experience. In the end, maybe it doesn't matter at all. I'd just like to know who to thank for altering my path. Life is worth living. Existing and living are not the same. Before my coma, I existed: I ate, slept, worked, and that was it. I kept my routine, but it was all meaningless. I now see that living means having love in your life, even with the messiness, complication, and pain it will cause. It is worth all the risks. So, no matter what the cause is for my experience, no matter how frightening it all was, I wouldn't trade it for anything, because now, I see.

THE AUTHOR

Madelyn March lives in a world of books. By day, she teaches children to read, and by night she can be found working on her next novel. In the moments between, she often daydreams of thought provoking plots and imagines ways to delve deeper into the psychology of her characters. She is fascinated with the power of a story to share the human experience in all its complexity.

Nature often plays an important part in Madelyn's stories. It's like a character in and of itself, so it's no surprise that when Madelyn is taking a moment to unplug, her favorite thing to do is hike in the Michigan forests with her family.

Madelyn is the author of the well-received novel, *The Nature of Denial.* Her third novel, *The Giving House,* will be released fall of 2017.

Learn more at madelynmarch.com.

....

Made in the USA
Monee, IL
22 November 2019